Pr

The Legend

"A fantastic work of dark l
Lansdale, Gorman, Pronzini, and McMurtry.
—Brian Keene, author of the *Rising* series

"Rountree excels at creating new mythology and folktales that feel like they've always existed, and *The Legend of Charlie Fish* is no exception. A tense, exciting, and gorgeous read that will sweep you up immediately and not let go, lingering even after you turn the last page."
—A. C. Wise, author of *Wendy, Darling*

"Equal parts touching and bizarre, *The Legend of Charlie Fish* is a Weird Western with heart and is a completely delightful read from start to finish."
—David Liss, author of *The Peculiarities*

"A winsome tale of wondrous misfits and unlikely kinships, *The Legend of Charlie Fish* channels all the wit and melancholy of the great Charles Portis. Part adventure story, part lament, the whole is a triumph of voice and heart."
—Andy Davidson, author of *The Hollow Kind*

"A tight heart-filled tapestry of almost alternate history that hits all the notes I crave in weird fiction. I adored it."
—John Boden, author of *Jedi Summer*, *Spungunion*, and *Snarl*

"Author Josh Rountree knows the city of Galveston and its tragic history backwards and forwards. Recommended for those who enjoy a good 'Weird Western.'"
—Nancy A. Collins, author of *Sunglasses After Dark*

"From the very first pages, Galveston and the Great Storm come alive alongside a cast of unique and compelling characters. The lyrical prose and sense of foreboding as undeniable as the first gusts of a hurricane make for an utterly charming and haunting tale."
—KC Grifant, author of *Melinda West: Monster Gunslinger*

"Josh Rountree has produced a fable from what we believe was a gentler time in history. . . . Beautifully written."
—Del Howison, author of *The Survival of Margaret Thomas*

"*The Legend of Charlie Fish* is an exciting mashup of historical Texas, whispering magic, deadly hurricanes, and unlikely friends from unexpected places."
—Patrick Swenson, author of *Rain Music*

"Odd, creepy, funny, *The Black Lagoon* meets the Six Gun universe. High up on the way-cool factor. You need this."
—Joe R. Lansdale, author of the *Hap and Leonard* series

"I was thoroughly taken with this story, Rountree's writing, and the unique island setting."
—*The Speculative Shelf*

"A Weird Western novel of singular power. Mix[es] equal parts of Elmore Leonard toughness and Joe R. Lansdale wit in a Charles Portis–shaped shaker."
—C. S. Humble, author of *The Massacre at Yellow Hill*

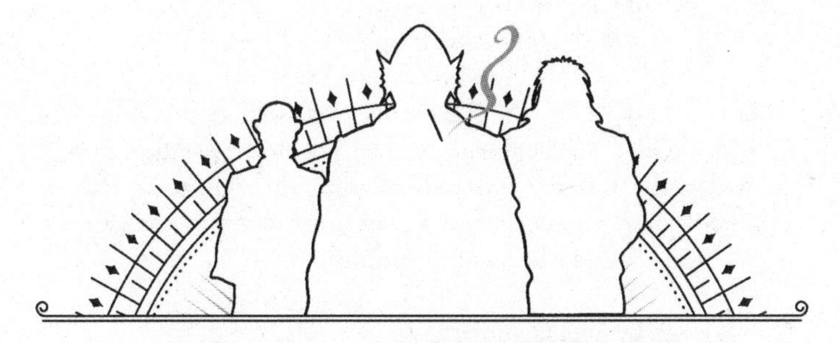

THE LEGEND OF CHARLIE FISH

TACHYON PUBLICATIONS
SAN FRANCISCO

The Legend of Charlie Fish

Cover design by John Coulthart
Interior design by Elizabeth Story
Author photo copyright © Leah Muse

Tachyon Publications LLC
1459 18th Street #139
San Francisco, CA 94107
415.285.5615
www.tachyonpublications.com
tachyon@tachyonpublications.com

Series editor: Jacob Weisman
Editor: Richard Klaw

Print ISBN: 978-1-61696-394-1
Digital ISBN: 978-1-61696-395-8

Printed in the United States by Versa Press, Inc.

First Edition: 2023
9 8 7 6 5 4 3 2 1

For Kristin.
Twenty-five years, and every day better than the last.

PROLOGUE: 1932

I LAY AWAKE in the dark, listening to ghosts.

The summer heat was furious, and hard rain sounded against the roof. An electric fan clattered and hummed but failed to offer any relief. My sleep clothes clung to my body, sodden with sweat, and I tossed on top of my sheets for an hour before giving up on sleep. When I turned on the bedside lamp, yellow light flooded the corners of my bedroom, and I walked barefooted to the window, looked out at the approaching hurricane.

I was not afraid of ghosts or of storms.

But they did make it hard to go to sleep.

Wind rattled the windows as I watched giant waves chip away at the beach. Black storm clouds crowded in from the Gulf, one after another. More than thirty years had passed since I first came to Galveston, since the greatest storm in memory had torn away the face of the old town and left it unrecognizable. There were few enough left who recalled the people and places stolen away by that storm, and when we passed one another on the streets, we saw reflections in each other's eyes of all we'd lost.

We understood hurricanes better now. Could more effectively predict their path and measure their ferocity.

But they were no less deadly.

Living on the island so long, I was no stranger to storms. But something about this one felt different. Light posts swayed beside the road, and palm trees gave up their fronds to the clawing wind. A couple of men stood along the seawall, hands on their hips, suitcoats flapping. The ocean felt heavy against the world, deep with secrets, and the wind carried voices I hadn't heard in a long time. Storms always stirred up the island's ghosts and they whispered in my head, anxious and insistent.

Even those who tended to keep quiet spoke up during storms.

I wished my brother was with me. I could hear his little-boy laughter and the bark of his pistol. I could smell gunpowder. I wished for another morning with Mr. Betts and Mrs. Elder, sitting around the breakfast table, listening to the sound of their quiet conversation, and Mrs. Elder's teaspoon rattling against her teacup as she stirred in a bit of milk. I wished for my father with his strong hugs, and my mother who held the key to every mystery I had never solved. Her most of all. Maybe she could help me rein in the ghosts, to figure out what they wanted. Help me finally tame the whisper talk that told me all the things I didn't want to know. Just thinking of her made the air smell like pine needles and burning sage, and I could feel three iron nails, cold in my hand. All their faces made reflections in the window, but it was just my imagination, a sort of wishful spell. The truth was, they were all gone.

Ghosts were my only company.

They crawled through the wet streets, hovered in the corners of my bedroom. They clung to the ceiling, dripping stagnant floodwater. The ghosts hounded me. People I'd lost, and those I'd never met. Some of them begged me to leave the island, but it was far too late for that. I had not meant to make a home in Galveston, but I'd been here so long, I wasn't sure where else I'd go. Others assured me it was time to die. It would be so easy to make a grave for myself and let the ocean rush to bury me. These were the voices that reminded me my death was overdue. I'd escaped it in childhood, and it had finally come for me. Whether I would escape it again, or whether I would take its hand willingly this time, even I wasn't certain.

I opened the window, and the wind rushed in like the house was gasping for breath.

Hot rain slicked the floor, and I could hear gulls struggling against the gale. The night growled and hissed. The air smelled like blood and rot, though I was sure that was only a memory come back to haunt me. Salt water burned my eyes and I breathed in the darkness. Dared the storm to come and take me. Whatever it wanted, I was ready to give this time. Ghosts tugged at my hair, placed cold whispering lips against my ears. Cried and pleaded and shrieked. But the ocean shouted loud enough to keep them at bay. I leaned out the second-story window, wondered if giving in to gravity would be the easiest surrender of all.

But then I heard Charlie.

Or not *heard* him, I suppose.

Charlie had been gone for decades, but every time the ocean grew angry, I could feel him pouring back into my mind, filling all the places that he'd left hollow. We were connected beyond all reason, and I wondered how often he felt me calling him from the depths. Did I haunt his thoughts the way he haunted mine? He felt so close. I leaned out farther, looked past the beach and out to sea, like I might see Charlie and his family, rising out of the misty darkness. Night swirled beyond the streetlights, but nothing else. Wind wrapped arms around me and pulled. But Charlie was there to hold me in place, his presence a sudden rush of cold water through my veins. I lurched away from the window. Could almost feel Charlie's scaled hands pulling me back to safety. His whispers in my head assured me death wasn't the answer, but neither was staying here. Charlie promised a better life, a better place.

He hadn't arrived yet, but he was really coming this time, and he was close.

I shut the window and listened to the muffled sound

of the wind pressing against the glass. Climbed back into bed, turned off the lamp.

And I slept peacefully after that, knowing one way or another, this would be my last night in Galveston.

FLOYD

We reached Galveston two days ahead of the storm.

It was a homecoming for me, but the children had never seen the ocean. The ferry cut through the water between the Bolivar Peninsula and the island, pitching like a cork in the swells. Nellie held tight to the railing with both hands, leaning as far as she dared toward the water. Hank stood behind her, gripping the back of his sister's dress.

"Is a storm coming?" Hank asked.

Low clouds obscured the horizon and colored the ocean a metallic gray. Hot winds tore in from the Gulf, causing men to clutch at their hats. The Texas flag snapped overhead like a bullwhip. Seagulls rode the surge, lighting on the boat for a time before allowing themselves to be lifted up again. They spun and dove, chased one another away beyond the line of smoke trailing behind the steam ferry.

"Looks like it'll rain, but nothing to worry about."

I'd lived a long time on the Gulf and was accustomed to the slow creep of tropical storms, but we'd had no indication that the weather intended any more than that.

"The captain is worried." Nellie turned and fixed me with a look that suggested she knew more about the situation than she was telling. The wind knotted her long blonde hair and worked diligently to lift the skinny girl into the air with the seagulls.

"Well, that's part of his job," I said. "Worrying about storms. But no reason you have to."

"Charlie Fish is uncomfortable."

"I imagine he is, but we can't help that right now."

Nellie stared at me with her pale-blue eyes until the hairs on my arm stood at attention. She had a habit of quickly changing conversation topics that I attributed to all the noise going on in her head. I hadn't believed Hank's stories about his sister's *whisper talk,* as he called it, until we brought Charlie Fish into the fold, and I saw the way they could communicate. Nellie had a way of *knowing* things that was more than a little unsettling.

"We should have given him a pillow," said Nellie.

"We don't have any pillows, Nellie," I said.

"And that tarp is scratchy against his back."

"We'll be there real soon, alright. He won't have to put up with it too much longer."

"How long before the next ferry?" she asked. "I expect those two scoundrels will be on it. They aren't going to let us be."

"You're turning my head in circles, girl. What is it

you want me to worry about? Storms or soft blankets or criminals?"

"I'm worried about it all," said Hank.

Nellie took her little brother's hand and he let her.

She was twelve and the boy was nine, and and if they hadn't told me, I'd never have guessed they were siblings. Nellie was tall as my shoulders, but Hank was short for his age and still wore the baby fat on his face. His hair was brown like river mud, and he dressed in rough wool pants with his cotton shirt always tucked in. A gun belt was cinched tight around his waist and the Peacemaker pistol he carried weighed near as much as he did. I'd witnessed the boy's skill with the weapon. Some might question him being allowed to roam around with his late father's gun on his hip, but they'd have to be the ones to take it from him.

My own father had left me nothing much of interest.

I'd traveled north to bury my namesake a few weeks earlier, alone, and returned home now with a pair of orphans and with Charlie Fish, whom we had to keep hidden. We'd helped him into the flatbed wagon, swaddled him in a tarp, and covered him with some grain bags before pulling the wagon onto the ferry. I told him to be as still as he could, and Nellie had a way of soothing him. So far, he'd kept quiet.

We'd had a bad encounter some days back with a pair of low-class men who'd captured Charlie, and they seemed like the sort who'd hunt him to perdition and beyond if necessary. I feared they'd turn up soon enough and something would have to be done.

The ferry moved across the bay, and the captain stirred everyone up with his nervous energy, barking about his barometer and the bruised color of the clouds and the way the wind pummeled the side of the ship like a lumbering bull. I was more worried about Professor Finn and Kentucky Jim than any hurricane. Storms were common in the summer. Worst case, it would pour for a while and flood the sidewalks, and you could always count on the rain to cool it down a few degrees.

Thankfully, the passage was short, and we reached Galveston Island without incident. The ferry docked not far from the main seaport, on the north side of the island, along the bay separating Galveston from the Texas mainland.

Nellie and Hank climbed onto the wagon, and I led the horses down from the ferry. Immigrants crowded this part of the pier. German and Spanish and other languages I couldn't recognize surrounded us as we rode past the campsites they'd erected along this stretch of the bay. Laughing children tossed rocks at passing steamers. Cookfires burned and hammers echoed out the sound of another building going up.

We made our way into the city proper, and up The Strand, a busy street that paralleled the bay. Two- and three-story buildings of brick and iron loomed over the street, made taller by the foot-high sidewalks built to keep floodwaters at bay. Bankers and builders and businessmen moved with the urgency of late afternoon, eager to finish whatever commerce drew them there. Electric lights hummed and cut yellow paths through the overcast gloom. Carriages jerked and clattered around us, and horses lashed to posts watched us pass, looking miserable. It was another burning hot September day and the intermittent rain had only intensified the humidity. Steam rose from the wet streets, fogging the windows.

Nellie and Hank absorbed the city with frank astonishment. They had lived their short lives in a small town in the middle of the piney woods and had never visited a city. Certainly not one so vital and alive as Galveston.

"This is where you live?" asked Hank.

"Near here," I said. "On the south side of town, closer to the beach."

"Do you know all these people?" he asked.

"No."

"It smells funny here."

"You're just not used to the ocean," I said.

"Is this where Charlie Fish is from? It smells like him."

"Stop bothering Mr. Betts," said Nellie. "He doesn't know where Charlie Fish is from."

Charlie remained covered. I'd have to take the horse and wagon back to the livery, but first I needed to get Charlie and the kids to Mrs. Elder's house.

We passed through downtown and crossed Broadway with its grassy esplanade and long stretch of stately mansions, guarded by iron fences and lush, tropical gardens. Farther south, colorful bungalows dominated the neighborhoods, and closer to the beach, houses stood on brick or wooden stilts to protect against heavy weather from the ocean. Doors and windows were left open to let the breeze off the water cool the homes, but the wind hammering in from the Gulf was hot and stifling.

Mrs. Elder's boarding house was a two-story wooden building a few blocks from the beach. Four brick-and-mortar columns lifted it about five feet off the ground, and a rickety staircase that I'd been promising to fix for a few months led down from the front door. The house had been painted bright yellow at one time, but the salty air had worn away the color until the gray, chipped boards underneath peeked through. I had been Mrs. Elder's only boarder when I left a couple of weeks ago, and I was hoping that was still the case.

"This is it," I said, stopping the wagon in the yard.

"Your house is tall," said Hank.

"It's not my house. I just live here."

"May I rouse Charlie Fish?" asked Nellie.

"Let him linger here for a bit," I said. "Probably better if I introduce you to Mrs. Elder first, and then we can bring him in. It's best if we prepare her."

"I think she'll love him," said Nellie.

"Yeah? Well, let's hope."

Abigail Elder was about my age, and a few strands of gray lightened her otherwise brilliant red hair. She had the energy and the manner of someone much younger, though we had the same tired creases at the corners of our eyes that would put lie to any claims of youth. She greeted us at the door and hugged Hank up against her with one arm. She put a hand on Nellie's shoulder and gave her a quick twirl.

"What a pretty thing you are!" she said.

"I'm Nellie Abernathy. Pleased to make your acquaintance, ma'am."

"And polite as a duchess. Now, what about this young man here? What's your name?"

"Hank."

"You an Abernathy too?"

"I'm her brother, ma'am."

"Well, come on in, Abernathy children. You too, Mr. Betts. I'll put some supper out. I expect y'all are hungry."

Mrs. Elder led us through the parlor and into the dining room where she'd already laid out a platter of fried chicken and a bowl of buttered biscuits. The smell of hot grease and flour caused my stomach to let loose with an animal growl and we tucked in at the table with a scrape of chair legs against Mrs. Elder's polished pine floor. The heavy crimson and gold drapery had been pulled aside to allow for some air, but the Gulf wind did little more than stir up the heat. We ate our food, sweating like the damned.

"Thank you, Mrs. Elder," I said. "This chicken is a wonder."

"Well, of course," she said. "You children like chicken?"

It was evident they did. Hank worked at a leg bone like he was desperate for every sinew, and even the normally demure Nellie devoured the chicken like it was her last meal. The children hadn't eaten well for some time, and that sort of hunger had a way of elevating a home-cooked meal to the level of a historic event.

"Yes, ma'am," said Hank, between bites. "Our mother fried it like this on Sundays sometimes."

Mrs. Elder gave me a meaningful look, and I knew she was politely waiting for me to explain these children I'd delivered to her doorstep. I had telegraphed her from Beaumont, so she wasn't entirely unprepared for our arrival, but I hadn't shared the details of how I'd acquired a pair of orphans, and I'd made no mention of Charlie Fish.

As if she plucked the thought from my mind—and it was a safe bet she had—Nellie tugged at my arm and said, "What about our friend?"

"I don't know if he eats chicken."

"What friend do you mean?" asked Mrs. Elder.

"Charlie Fish," said Nellie. "He's still in the wagon."

I had hoped to at least finish our meal before having to make my explanations, but Nellie was obviously having none of it.

"Mr. Betts?" said Mrs. Elder. "Are there more children?"

"No more children, but . . . well, I thought maybe I would approach the introduction of Charlie Fish with a bit of delicacy. I didn't want to shock you."

"I'm not a delicate woman, Mr. Betts. And I've seen enough that I'm rarely shocked."

"Charlie is hiding under a tarp," said Hank, pulling a

chicken wing in half. "Mr. Betts figured it's best if nobody sees him."

"Have you brought a criminal to my home?" asked Mrs. Elder.

"No, nothing like that," I said.

"Then you should invite your friend inside. The rain is picking up again."

I could hear it, tapping against the roof, and I could smell salt from the ocean.

"Explain to her, Mr. Betts. She won't object." Nellie smiled at me, and bit into a biscuit.

"Okay, then. The short of it is, these two children were in need of assistance, and I wasn't sure what else to do but to bring them along with me. And we . . . well, we met Charlie Fish along the way, and he required assistance also."

"We rescued him from scoundrels," said Nellie.

"And we don't want them to find him again," said Hank. "Also, he looks like a fish, so he might scare some folks."

Mrs. Elder wore a bemused expression that I found very familiar. I'd earned her vexation enough times in the two years I'd been her boarder to recognize when it was aimed at someone else.

"A fish?" Mrs. Elder's fingers worked absently at the yellowed lace table cover, flattening the creases. She'd told me once it had been her grandmother's, and that was one of the few personal things she'd ever shared. She had never mentioned her husband, so I presumed her a widow, but I'd never asked her for details.

"Sort of like if a man was a fish," said Hank.

"But he's not an animal," said Nellie. "And he's very smart."

I wasn't sure what Mrs. Elder was making of all this, but she had a way of taking things as they came.

"Well, Mr. Betts," she said, "I need to meet this Charlie Fish. How about you invite him inside?"

"I'll call him," said Nellie.

Mrs. Elder watched Nellie expectantly, like she was waiting for the girl to holler out to Charlie, but I knew what the girl meant. She was calling him, but not with her voice.

"Are you going to get him?" Mrs. Elder asked.

"He's coming," said Nellie.

The front door opened, and we could hear the rain picking up outside. Footsteps sounded on the floorboard, wet and squeaky, and the room smelled like the wharves, like fishing boats after they'd returned from a long time at sea. Charlie Fish crossed the parlor and stood framed in the dining room doorway, still clutching the tarp tight around him. Even in the early September evening, when the sun would hang on to near nine o'clock, the cloud cover left the room dim enough that I couldn't quite make out the face peering out from the folds of the tarp.

"Charlie, this is Mrs. Elder." Nellie spoke as if she were introducing a pair of acquaintances at a church luncheon. "This is her house and she's a friend. You'll be safe here for a while."

Mrs. Elder stood to receive her guest, an apron still

wrapped around her midsection to protect her blue-and-white gingham dress. When Charlie Fish let the tarp fall to the floor, she dropped back into her chair like a sack of flour.

"Please don't take fright," I said. "Charlie isn't dangerous."

He stood all of seven feet with arms and legs just like any of us, but blue-and-green scales covered him entirely, like a suit of armor. He scanned the room with bulbous black eyes that refused to settle on any one thing, and his mouth was wide and red, like someone had taken a knife and cut a gash nearly ear to ear. Gills fanned out on either side of his head, blowing smoke like a steam engine. He'd dug out a cigarette from my pack and held it awkwardly in one clawed hand, lifting it repeatedly to his mouth like he had a nervous condition. Charlie had taken to smoking like he was an old hand, despite Nellie's constant admonitions about it being a nasty practice. The girl had practically chased me away from the habit by this point, but Charlie Fish was stubborn.

He looked wiry under all those scales, and he moved in a rubbery fashion that made it hard to figure out where all his bones were. But he was strong; I'd seen him lift the back of the wagon when we'd gotten stuck in some mud, and I wouldn't want to have to fight him.

I'd provided him a pair of my long johns to wear—he had more than arms and legs in common with men, and modesty demanded it—but otherwise we hadn't found any clothes to fit him. The long johns fit tight as a second skin and stopped mid-shin. I was near six feet tall, but Charlie was a tower.

"Charlie, it's not polite to smoke in someone's house!" Nellie looked scandalized. Red blossomed across her face, and I could tell she was pushing back at whatever instinct had driven Charlie to announce himself in such a manner.

Charlie dropped the half-smoked cigarette to the floor and squashed it out with his large, webbed foot.

"Charlie, you can't do that!" said Nellie.

He made a wet bleating sound that we'd come to understand was his way of speaking, and he nodded like he was agreeing to something the rest of us couldn't hear.

"I'm sorry." Nellie got up from the table, crossed over to Charlie, and put a hand on his arm. "He doesn't know any better, but he's learning."

"Well, as long as he doesn't smoke inside, he's welcome to stay for a while." Mrs. Elder shook her head, as if trying to clear away the fog of what she was seeing. She'd been momentarily flattened by the sight of the fish man, but she was regaining herself in a hurry.

"You don't seem quite as shocked as I imagined you'd be," I said.

"Oh, I'm shocked," said Mrs. Elder. "But I'm no skeptic, Floyd Betts. What kind of hubris would it take to believe there's nothing beyond the natural world as we know it?"

"Well, he shocked me when I met him."

"There's stranger things in Texas than Charlie Fish,

I know that much. My mother used to tell stories about wolf people roaming the hills up near Austin when she was a girl, and there's not a building in San Antonio that isn't home to a ghost. I met a lady some years back who used to listen to their stories and write them down. I figure your friend here is just something we haven't discovered before now. The way I see things is, if the Creator saw fit to put something in the world, then it's here for a reason. Who am I to question that?"

"Charlie appreciates your hospitality," said Nellie.

"He doesn't want anything to eat?"

"He's not hungry."

"Well, we can find him a bed for the night, at least," said Mrs. Elder. "And Mr. Betts?"

"Ma'am?"

"Take your horse and wagon to the livery, but when you get back, I'm going to have some questions for you."

When I returned from the livery, we walked the children to the beach.

The streets on this part of the island climbed as they approached the shore, making it seem like the neighborhood was situated in a giant bowl waiting to be filled. The beach itself wasn't even visible until you crested the last block and the ocean opened up along the horizon, but you could hear waves crashing and gulls crying well before the water came into view. The shoreline extended for miles in both directions, straining against the constant weight of the ocean as it churned up against the continent.

Night had fallen, but the bathhouses and ramshackle businesses selling fried seafood, seashell keepsakes, and cold drinks were illuminated by electric lights strung up on poles that swayed in the wind. Trolleys rode wooden trestles over the sand, and tourists and locals alike splashed in the swells.

Nellie and Hank kept a respectful distance from the ocean; Hank had rolled up his pants legs to his knees just in case he worked himself up to going in the water, while Nellie had left her shoes alongside the road and dug her toes in the sand.

Mrs. Elder and I sat down on a stone bench and watched the children edge closer to the sea, daring one another to be the first to put a toe in the lapping waves. The rain had stopped for a time, but the wind and the heat still beat against the island and Mrs. Elder sat with her hands firmly on her dress to keep it from blowing up. I told her in broad strokes how I'd come upon the children, about our first encounter with Charlie Fish, and the men who were likely still hunting for him.

Men who might follow us to her doorstep.

"You had quite a trip," she said.

"I did, in fact."

"And your plan for the children? Do you have one?"

"I haven't had time to sort that matter to my satisfaction. They needed help and I provided it. Haven't figured what to do next. There's the orphanage. That's one option."

Just up the beach stood a decaying brick building that served as an orphanage. I had every confidence that the sisters there would take better care of these kids than I could, but something about leaving them to wander those dark halls after what they'd gone through didn't sit well with me.

"I never had any children of my own," said Mrs. Elder. "Always wanted some, but circumstances conspired against me, I'm afraid. I believe I'd have made an adequate mother, given the chance. Maybe a good one."

"I'm sure you would have."

"What I think I'm saying is, if you don't want to make a decision yet, there's no reason to. There's room in the boarding house for the children, and for Charlie Fish besides. There's no need to take any actions in haste."

She sat close beside me as she spoke, and I felt hollowed out by sadness. I had never considered long on what it was I wanted in life, beyond managing day by day to stay above ground, but Mrs. Elder painted a tempting picture with her talk of all of us living under one roof. Others on the beach could have mistaken us for a married couple enjoying the early evening with our children. It was the kind of family life that I'd never experienced, and honestly never much considered. But I had grown fond of the children in our short time together, and I'd already been fond of Mrs. Elder. All that said, it wasn't a family that Mrs. Elder was offering, and I would be wrong to presume anything so grand. Still, it was a home for the children, for a time at least.

"I wouldn't want to endanger you," I said.

Mrs. Elder gave me a grim smile. "Maybe those men will find you and maybe they won't. I'm not afraid of men who put on like they're bigger than they are. They come to my door, they might find I'm more than they want to deal with."

I suspected she was right.

"You also have the problem of Charlie Fish to sort out," she said. "There's no orphanage for one like him."

"Nellie says he wanted to come to Galveston with us," I said. "I half expected him to jump right in the ocean and swim away when we got here."

Charlie had wanted to come with us to the beach, but Nellie had admonished him to stay out of sight. He'd watched us leave with a powerful longing, but he hadn't followed.

"Well, he can stay a while too, but I think you'll have a problem keeping him hid for long."

"I'll just add that to my list of situations I've got to sort out."

"That list is getting long," she said.

"That list started out long."

"Well, you might want to scribble down *hurricane* there at the bottom somewhere," she said.

"Weather's not going to be that bad, is it?"

"Not if you ask the weather service," she said. "I walked up there this morning and they're saying heavy wind and rain for the next few days. Maybe a little flooding, but not much more than that. I think they might be wrong, though. I've lived on this island a long time. Way the wind's swirling, it's got some kind of teeth. Like it's coming from the ocean and the bay all at once. Wind like that will nibble on you for a while, but soon enough it's liable to take a great big bite."

I'd endured heavy weather on the island before, and I believed the city was prepared for it.

Hurricanes and floods were no match for Galveston, Texas. The strong piers sunk deep in the sand, the wooden bathhouses, all the elevated homes and the stoutly constructed buildings along The Strand: they invited the weather to do its worst. The city had raced out ahead of so many others, seemingly arriving at the brink of the new century much more quickly than its peers. Iron and brick and steel and electricity joined together to tame the land, and Galveston was poised to rival any East Coast city that cared to accept the challenge.

Never mind pretenders to the throne like Houston.

Ask anyone on the island, and they'd agree. Hurricanes were a nuisance, but no real threat to a city like Galveston.

"Well, I suspect Charlie Fish would enjoy a hurricane," I said.

"Maybe the hurricane will blow away my front steps and save you the trouble of fixing them."

"I'm sorry I haven't gotten to that."

Mrs. Elder laughed. "You've had enough on your plate, sounds like."

"I appreciate your offer to let the children and Charlie stay for a bit while I figure this out. That sounds like a fine idea."

Neither of the children went more than ankle-deep into the water, but on our walk back to the boarding house both of them threatened to go in up to their knees the next time.

Mrs. Elder put the children in the empty bedroom next to hers, and it was decided that even though there was another room to spare, Charlie Fish would bunk with me.

We fixed him a pallet of blankets on the floor by the window so he could hear the waves. I'd never seen him sleep much, but he curled up in the blanket and whistled quietly through his gills as I got in bed and put out the lantern.

Sometime during the night, I woke and saw Charlie standing there in front of the window, looking out toward the beach. The ocean hammered the island. It was a constant low rumble that I could feel in the walls, like something massive was slowly burrowing underneath us. Rain spattered in through the open window, beading on Charlie's scales. He put his hands on the windowsill, leaned out a few inches to test the night. He seemed to be searching for something beyond the shoreline. Beyond the horizon.

I didn't need Nellie to tell me what he was looking for.

NELLIE

On the day my brother and I became orphans, our mother sent us to gather ingredients for a spell. Some of these things, like bog hemp and duckweed, we found downriver from the mill, where the water tunneled through shadows and towering pines. For the rest, we'd need to visit Mr. O'Casey's general store and endure his frank disapproval, so we delayed that meeting for as long as possible. We removed our shoes and let our feet sink into the mud, laughing and splashing in the shallows. We chased squirrels up cypress trees and tried to throw pine-cones across the river. And when we eventually trudged back into town, our pockets full of plants, we climbed the steps to that general store like two children on their way to the gallows.

A tarnished brass bell rang overhead as we opened the door. Mr. O'Casey stood behind a countertop crowded with jars of penny candies and cigars. The shelves behind him warped beneath the weight of dry goods, coils of baling wire, tin kerosine canisters, and questionable medicines.

"Good afternoon, Mr. O'Casey," I said. "I hope you're having an enjoyable day."

Mr. O'Casey gave us a look that indicated how delighted he'd be to see us drowned in the river. "There's very little to enjoy about it."

"Well, perhaps the evening time will be better." Mother had taught me that dealing with unpleasant people was no cause to abandon our manners.

"Why have you come?" He gripped the countertop with both hands, like a preacher at the pulpit. My brother, Hank, slid Mother's handwritten list across the counter, and Mr. O'Casey picked it up, peered at it through his wire spectacles. He mouthed the words of every item as he read it. His face was drawn and sweaty, and he'd slicked his hair to the side with so much pomade, it looked like he'd lathered it in lard. I stood still as a statue while he considered the list, and did my best not to react to the rank, animal smell of the man.

"What do you need all this for?" he asked.

"What does that matter?" asked Hank.

"Don't be rude, Hank," I said.

"I don't like him much," said Hank.

"Even so."

"I don't conduct business with disrespectful children." Mr. O'Casey tossed the list back at Hank, hissed through his teeth, and crossed his heart. "Especially witchy ones like you."

"We're neither of those things," I said. "And we've brought plenty of money."

I removed the small canvas bag Mother had given us, showed Mr. O'Casey the money. If nothing else, I knew his avarice would outweigh his hatred for our family. I considered reaching out with my whisper talk, trying to place some kindness toward us in his mind, but I didn't want to engage with him in that way, and besides, his thoughts were already spilling over into my own, cold and inescapable. He imagined my mother, naked and tied to a stake. Burning. Screaming. He imagined other, horrible things he might do to her before setting her ablaze. I kept a smile on my face, grinding my teeth together to keep from crying, until finally he relented and went about packaging up our list of supplies.

A plug of Carolina tobacco.

A pint of grain alcohol.

Three iron nails.

Hank and I waited in the hot, swampy interior of the general store while Mr. O'Casey gathered everything. We endured his commentary with feigned good humor.

"Goes against my better judgement to sell you people anything," he said.

"Well, you're kind to do it," I said.

"Count yourself lucky."

"Blessed, more like."

"Are you making fun of me, girl?"

"No, sir," I said. "I'd never."

"Because you can take your business all the way to Houston if you are."

"I know to respect my elders, Mr. O'Casey."

He grunted and turned back to his shelves. Hank fumed beside me, boring holes into the back of Mr. O'Casey's skull with his stare.

"I'll walk to Houston," Hank whispered.

"Shush. It's a long way."

"How far?"

"Too far for you," I said.

"You don't know how far I can walk."

"Hank, hush!"

Mr. O'Casey turned back toward us. Hank didn't bother to hide his disdain, but Mr. O'Casey had already seen the color of our money and I knew he wouldn't turn it down. I counted out coins, put them in his hand, and he passed the wares across the counter to me.

"Tell your mother to be mindful of how she makes use of these items," he said.

"I'm sure she will be."

I didn't mistake his meaning. He didn't want her to make any more of her remedies. Mr. O'Casey had a large selection of supposed medicines in brown glass bottles, all of them lined up straight as tin soldiers on the shelves. They purported to fix any ailment from toothaches to consumption, though Father had told us they were mostly alcohol flavored with sugar and plants. Mr. O'Casey bought them from a traveling salesman who came through town in a wagon every so often, then he raised the cost as soon as the salesman had gone. No matter, the people of Old Cypress were ready customers, except for those who discovered Mother's homemade remedies.

Mother's remedies were far more effective.

That was reason enough for Mr. O'Casey to spread rumors about her, to question what dark bargain a witch like her had struck to create such impossible potions. After all, she was a woman who went about town in her bare feet, with her hair unbound, hanging long and golden down her back. She wore a necklace of flowers and spent long afternoons alone in nature. Mother was often spotted walking alone at night, and our homelife was unconventional. Mr. O'Casey had convinced quite a few folks that Mother was a witch.

And he was right, of course.

But he never really understood what that meant.

"Our business is concluded," he said. "Scat."

My mother continued to burn in Mr. O'Casey's thoughts, and I started to tremble. The whispers in my mind overtook my cautious nature. Mother would have told me to leave well enough alone, but I couldn't help myself. I reached out into his thoughts and plucked her from that fire like I was picking a daisy from the garden, then I replaced her with Mr. O'Casey himself. Knotted tight to a post, ropes digging into his skin. Fire chasing up his legs. Everyone in town gathered around his burning body, chanting. *Witch, witch, witch.* And Mr. O'Casey, the *real* Mr. O'Casey, yelped and backed away in a hurry, like I was a snake he'd spotted lurking in the leaves. His medicine bottles rattled together as he stumbled against the shelves. One of them fell to the floor and shattered, and the smell of whiskey blossomed in the air.

"Have a pleasant afternoon." I grabbed Hank's hand and pulled him along behind me. We left the store in a hurry.

Outside, the air smelled like cut logs, and men shouted instructions at one another as they loaded lumber onto a flatbed wagon in front of the sawmill. A half dozen children kicked a leather ball around in front of the whiskey bar. Horses stomped about in a small corral next to the livery, and the sound of a hammer against an anvil echoed through the town. The dark curtain of pine trees that surrounded us held everything close—the shouting, the heat, the wet stench of the horses and the muddy street. A pair of squat men with heavy beards and pistol belts stood by the corral. They talked among themselves and watched us leave the general store. Their thoughts itched at my mind. Not for the first time I wished I could turn the whisper talk off, but I couldn't help but catch the terrible things they were thinking about us.

I pulled Hank closer to me as we started up the street and hurried toward home.

We were unloved in Old Cypress. Outsiders, though Hank and I had never known any other place. Our father had lived there most of his life, apart from the two years he left after his parents died. *Escaped* is how he described it. But Old Cypress had a way of holding on to its own, and when he came back home, he brought my mother with him, and me in her belly, and they hadn't bothered to lie when people asked them about their union. I mean to say, they weren't married, were never married. And Mother wasn't the sort of woman Preacher Cuthbert would welcome in the church on Sunday mornings.

Not that she had any desire to go.

Hank picked up a stick and clattered it against the iron fence that surrounded the churchyard, hitting every bar as we walked past it.

"That's impolite," I said. "Put that stick down."

"Maybe I just ain't polite," he said.

"That much is for certain."

"Not like I could hurt this fence anyways," he said. "Whole place looks like it might fall down if somebody gave it a good kick."

He wasn't wrong. The church looked uncared for by its parishioners. I didn't care for it either, but that had more to do with the people inside the building than anything having to do with busted siding and broken windows. Father told us a lot of good people go to church, and Mother agreed, but she added that none of them went to *that* church, and hers was a hard point to argue. During the week, the church sanctuary served as the local schoolhouse, but Mother said there was nothing they were teaching that she wanted us to learn, and so she taught us at home.

"When are we leaving?" Hank asked.

"Soon," I said. "A week or so."

"Do they have catfish in California?" Hank's stick

clattered against the last iron fence bar, then he started swinging it around like a sword.

"I don't know what kind of fish they have," I said.

"Hopefully not just perch. Catfish taste better than perch."

"You'll probably have all manner of fish to choose from," I said. "California is right next to the Pacific Ocean."

"Texas has an ocean too," he said. "Why do we need to go all the way to California for that?"

"Because California is a long way from here."

When our parents had decided it was time to leave Old Cypress, I don't think the ocean had anything to do with their planning. California wasn't any place special to them. Just a spot on the map. But it was west, about as far west as you could go, and that horizon had been calling people to it, for better or worse, ever since the Europeans had landed and set up shop in the original colonies. There was something magical about California, and Father insisted he could find work there, that they could be happy there. That even Mother might be accepted there, at least in some small way. And it was hard to imagine California could be anything but a step up from Old Cypress. Our parents had been planning our departure for months, and were close to leaving, but the residents of Old Cypress seemed to sense a change in our manner, and while they certainly wanted us gone, there was an element among them that wanted us to pay a price for leaving.

Their anger was hot. I could feel it, and so could

Mother. She was never able to hide much from me, and I knew she was afraid something bad would happen before we were ready to go.

Thus, the trip to town. Thus, the spell.

The day we rode out of Old Cypress would be the happiest day of my life.

"Catfish tastes good over a fire," said Hank, "but it's best when you put a little cornmeal on it and fry it in a pan. I don't know if they have catfish or cornmeal either one in California."

"We'll know soon enough."

"I'm not sure I want to go," he said.

"Why not?" I asked. "You hate it here."

"Yeah, but I might hate California too. At least here, I know they have cornmeal. And biscuits."

I wasn't sure how to explain to him what it would mean for our family to stay in Old Cypress. The town was rusted and moldy and grim. Like it had caught some wasting disease, and no one was willing to administer the cure. Mother had explained to me the concept of entropy, how if something stops moving forward it would start to die. That's what happened to Old Cypress. That's what was happening to the people here. And I knew I didn't want to die with them. There was nothing for us here, and I still didn't understand why my father had moved back in the first place.

"I expect they'll have all that and more," I said.

"They better, else we'll have to keep on until we find someplace that does."

Hank was afraid of Old Cypress, but he was more afraid of leaving. It came at me like a bright red sensation behind my eyes. I hated that Hank couldn't hide that fear from me, no matter how much little boy bluster he summoned, but the ability to read his emotions was in my blood. Mother called it *seeing inside* and I called it *whisper talk*, but it amounted to the same thing, an ability passed down through the generations—grandmother to mother to daughter, and so on—all the way back to the beginning of time as far as I knew, an ability that allowed you to know things you weren't supposed to know, to understand what people were thinking, and sometimes, to anticipate things that hadn't happened yet.

Mother called it a gift, but if so, it was one I wished I'd never been given.

We reached the edge of Old Cypress proper, where a few broken-down houses sat lodged in the arms of encroaching pines, and I could still feel the weight of the town's disdain, pressing up against my back. Mr. O'Casey, the millworkers, the children with their shrill laughter, and the dour men with their pistols; all those thoughts and designs came together in one inescapable notion.

We were different, and different was bad.

Hank and I set off down the road to home, and their hatred chased after us.

We lived about a half mile from town, in a house that had belonged to my late grandparents. Our father loved that house, knew every inch and angle of it. He'd learned to farm on the few acres of land that his grandfather had cleared around it, and he'd kept the home even when he left for what he'd hoped were greener pastures. He'd come back to start his family here, and I could feel the pride of place warring with the pain of knowing he had to leave it, to keep us all safe. It was a simple clapboard house with a loft on one side, where Hank and I slept, and a screened-in front porch. Father kept it whitewashed and in fine working order. Hank and I stomped up the steps onto the porch, and we knew Father was home because the gun belt with his heavy Peacemaker pistol hung from the hook on the porch, next to the door. He'd taken to carrying it with him anytime he left, thanks to our deteriorating relationship with the people in town, but Mother wouldn't allow it in the house. Father's squirrel rifle always occupied a nook beside the stone hearth inside, but Mother had a special dislike for pistols, so the Peacemaker stayed on the porch.

Mother had every window open to let in any breeze that cared to show itself, but the house was still an oven. She had her hair tied back and the sleeves of her dress rolled up to her elbows. She was ready for us. A cast-iron pot occupied the center of our dining table, and a box of matches sat beside it. Her spell book lay open nearby. The book had been handed down for ages, and I knew I'd have it someday, whether I wanted it or not. My late grandmother was nothing to me but a sad-eyed lady who watched the proceedings from a photograph on the mantle, and a cautionary tale that being a witch was a dangerous avocation, one that did not always align with a person's desire to find out what old age was like.

Hank and I put our packages on the table, emptied our pockets of everything we'd gathered.

"You've come home," Mother said. "I thought for sure you'd run away and set sail for the Cliffs of Dover."

"We encountered some delays." I grinned when I said it, understanding already that Mother knew every step we'd taken, and was only teasing.

"No one gave you trouble?" Father stood like a grim shadow next to Mother, bone-tired and eager to be gone.

"Nobody but that smelly grocer," said Hank.

"He barely troubled us," I said.

"He troubled us some," said Hank.

"Not enough to matter."

"He didn't lay a hand on you, did he?" asked Father.

"No, and he wouldn't."

Everyone understood my meaning. Mr. O'Casey had no particular aversion to punishing children—his or anyone else's—but his fear of Mother ran cold in his blood, and I didn't think he had the nerve to overcome it.

I didn't think so *then*, anyway.

"Well, I'm sorry for however he behaved," Father said. "You children shouldn't have to put up with that sort of nonsense. A grown man hectoring children."

"Don't apologize for things that aren't your fault." Mother put a hand on the back of Father's neck, and I could see the tension drain out of him like water through a sluice. "We'll be gone soon enough, and all these miserable people can just keep on being miserable without us. Nellie, if you'll help me, let's get this spell sorted so we can have some dinner and think about more pleasant things."

She didn't need my help, but everything between us was some form of instruction. She watched as I put the plants we'd collected into the pot and formed them into something resembling a nest. Mother had already assembled some other ingredients, taken from the mason jars she kept shelved in the root cellar—animal bones and acorns and yellow plants I didn't recognize—and she added these things to the pile. She measured out a bit of the tobacco, added it to the mix, then dumped the full pint of alcohol over the top of it all.

Finally, she placed the three nails in the pot, arranged together in a triangle.

"We don't have precisely what we need here, but precision isn't necessary," Mother said. "It's as much about intent as anything else."

"Will it work?" I asked.

"Magic always works," Mother said, "just not always the way you expect it to."

Mother picked up the matchbook, handed it to me.

"Cast the spell, Nellie," she said.

I will always remember the smell of alcohol and the rasp of the match as I drew it across the tabletop. I will always remember the firelight reflected in my mother's eyes, and the proud smile on her face as I read aloud the words from her book, as I willed the protection spell into existence.

And I will always wonder if I did something wrong.

The pot burned with a green, unnatural light. The deep afternoon shadows retreated to the corners of the room as the fire lunged and swayed. It burned silent and cold, and the temperature dropped so fast I could see my breath in front of my face. We watched together without speaking, even Hank, until the fire died out. Then Mother reached into the embers with a set of metal tongs, removed the three iron nails, and laid them out on the hearth to cool. We ate cold leftovers for dinner, the four of us laughing and joking, not at all like people who were being chased from their home. A family, no matter the circumstances. Then, while Hank and I cleaned up, Mother and Father took the nails out onto the porch. Father hammered them into the top of the doorframe, one by one, so that no ill will could cross that threshold.

When Hank and I climbed up into our loft that evening, I had a hard time sleeping. The heat never relented that time of year in Texas, even at night, and my sleep clothes were soaked in sweat. Hank was uncomfortable too, and he asked if I'd sleep on the porch with him. He was afraid to go by himself. So, I grabbed my pillow and followed him outside. It wasn't uncommon to sleep on the porch in those days, during the hottest months. The night certainly wasn't cool, but there was just enough breeze so that you could breathe.

Once we settled in on the porch, we were both asleep in a hurry.

I dreamed of fire. Green and red and blue. Black smoke

coiled up like a snake, ready to strike. I dreamed of hard eyes, laughing children, and tin canisters of kerosene. And I dreamed that the whole dirty town of Old Cypress was overrun by a wall of water like nothing ever seen on earth, a bright silver rush so angry and intense that nothing but bricks and splinters remained when it had passed. If I'd been able to will that torrent into the waking world, I might well have done it, but when Hank shook me and roused me from sleep, it wasn't the water he was screaming about, but the fire.

"Wake up, Nellie! Wake up!"

"Hank. What?"

I wasn't sure I was awake at first, but my eyes were wide open. The heat was a monstrous, living thing, and the flames were so bright it felt like the sun had swallowed up the earth. Hank pulled at my arm, trying to get me off the porch. Smoke pressed down on top of us, burned my eyes. When I looked up, I saw those three nails Father had hammered into the door frame, glowing like miniature red stars. Fire poured in shimmering waves from the doorway, engulfed the walls and the roof of the covered porch. There was no way to get inside, no option to do anything but crawl down the steps on our hands and knees and run out into the field before we burned to death.

The smoke started us coughing, and already my skin felt burned like I'd spent all day out in the sun. Hank was crying and shouting something at me, but my head was buzzing, and I couldn't hear what he was trying to say. He had hold of Father's pistol belt with the gun still in the holster; the only thing he loved besides me that he'd escaped with.

I could feel *everything* happening in the house, and there was nothing to do but endure it. I buried my face in the dirt, screaming, and Hank held me there until the fire burned down and the sun came up.

Nobody from town came to see what happened.

I figured that's because they already knew.

FLOYD

TWO WEEKS before I brought the children home to Galveston, I rode out to bury my father.

My Aunt Constance had telegraphed to tell me he was dead and that she had no intention of paying to bury him, so if I didn't want him left somewhere for the animals to gnaw on, I had better come and tend to matters. I knew she wasn't bluffing. Constance was a hard woman, and she disliked my father even more than I did. The telegram hadn't told me how he died, but I half suspected Constance had finally murdered him.

I hired a horse and wagon for the trip in case I needed to haul anything back with me, and it had been handy, just not in the way I'd expected.

My father lived more than half his life in a town called Old Cypress that was buried so deep in the swamp and pine trees that you could spend most days there and never get one good look at the sun. Some of the land had been carved out for farming, and a fair number of the men in the area made their living cutting trees, but nature always had a way of creeping back no matter how hard you fought against it. Branch and leaf and slithering vine all eager to climb up out of that sodden earth and overgrow anything that stayed in one spot for too long.

Riding back into that place felt like a surrender.

The summer heat hugged the ground, and all those trees kept it trapped there like steam in a boiler. No wind moved through, but living things rustled the underbrush and splashed in the black stream that ran alongside the road. It smelled like leaves left for ages to molder, of stagnant water and my own sweat. The wagon shuddered over the uneven dirt road, and the horse had slowed his pace like he was working his way through a pool of molasses. When the road turned and Old Cypress finally came into view, the horse quickened his step, more eager to get where we were going than I was.

The main part of town consisted of a dozen buildings in a large clearing—the sawmill where my father had worked when I was young right along the riverbank, a general goods store, a combination blacksmith and livery, a falling down church, a couple of whiskey halls, and various other businesses. Most of the houses were built around the edges of town in haphazard fashion. The streets were little more than muddy paths.

Decay had hold of the buildings. Nothing but splintered, whitewashed wood and a few bits of crumbling brick and stone that had been hauled in from God knows where. Rust pocked nearly every bit of metal—

the creaking fence that surrounded the churchyard, the troughs at the livery, the work bell hanging at the mill. Dark mold climbed the walls and covered the roofs.

Decay had hold of the people too. It was midday when I rode into town, and few raised their eyes to see who was arriving. They slunk around like people set at some terrible task that demanded more than they could give. A couple of old men sat out in front of the general store smoking cigarettes, and even this seemed too much a burden. They watched me approach through rising heat waves, eyes glazed and faces bent up like they'd smelled a corpse. Everyone looked tired and miserable, and I was starting to remember how that town had a way of pressing down on you until you felt your life escaping like smoke from a chimney.

My father's house, a place I'd left when I was fifteen and hadn't seen since, stood at the edge of the tree line not far from the mill. Aunt Constance watched me rein up in the yard, standing in the doorway like she was afraid I meant to move in and claim the place. Sawdust filtered down through the air and insects rattled in the trees.

"Well, you come home then," she said. "You've aged a mite, ain't you?"

"It's been more than twenty years."

"Say it has?"

"Yes, ma'am."

"Don't seem that long."

"You look just about the same to me."

And she did. Her hair had gone white, and she stood

with more of a stoop, but her face was still sharp like a Bowie knife, and she was so thin you could practically see through her. She stood with one hand on her hip and the other gripping the front door, which looked like it had lost the bottom hinge and was starting to pull away from the top one. She wore a faded green dress I remember belonging to my mother, and I'm sure she picked it out that day on purpose.

Constance squinted at me, like she couldn't tell if I was being sincere or intending some insult.

"You'll find that life don't get no easier the older you get," she said. "Just misery heaped on top of misery until you die."

"Well, I have that to look forward to, I guess."

Constance looked at me like I was making her head hurt. "Your Daddy's body is laid out over at the church. Already in the coffin with his shoes shined and his hair combed. Preacher just needs you to pay and they'll put him in the ground right there in the churchyard next to your mother. He's asking ten dollars, so I hope you have it."

"I've got the money."

"Good," she said. "I'll walk you over there. You can pay the man and then turn yourself back around to Galveston."

"I'd like to go inside," I said. "Just real quick."

"You don't need nothing in here," she said. "This is my house now. You ain't taking nothing with you, so don't even ask."

There was nothing of hers I wanted. Nothing of my

father's that I wanted except for maybe his carpentry tools, and I was sure Constance had sold those off by now along with anything else he owned that would fetch a few dollars.

"I left some books behind," I said. "Let me get those and we can finish all this business today. I'll leave and you and me can go back to missing one another."

"You were always smart, weren't you?"

I didn't know if she meant smart like being disrespectful, or smart like being intelligent. Didn't matter much. She wouldn't care for either one.

Finally, she stood aside and waved me toward the door, heaving a sigh like having to deal with me was too much weight on her soul.

Inside the house, it was nearly too hot to breathe. Constance had all the windows closed and the curtains pulled. A pair of old rockers sat beside the hearth, and I could still see my parents sitting in them, side by side, a memory from some ancient time before my mother died and everything went awry. The room that had been mine was filled with stacked-up furniture, empty mason jars, bolts of moldy fabric, a guitar with no strings; like everything nobody needed had been put in one room and sealed away. Beneath a faded and food-stained tablecloth, I found the stack of books my mother had brought with her from Tennessee when we'd first moved to Texas. Just ten or twelve worn leather volumes draped in spiderwebs, but that was as good as a library in a place like Old Cypress.

"Why do you want them books?" Constance stood a

close watch, like she figured I might shove something of value in my pockets while she wasn't looking.

"Did you have plans to read them?"

"You never know," she said. "I might get bored."

"They belonged to my mother." I clutched the stack of books against my chest and made like I was ready to leave.

"That don't mean nothing to me," she said. "I never liked her no more than I liked you. No more than I liked my lazy brother. You didn't even ask me how he died. Drank too much and fell off his horse. Cracked his head open on a rock. That's about the kind of death he deserved, I figure. Them books, they might be worth some money."

"I'm going to take these books with me," I said. "And if you don't agree to that, then you can find ten dollars to bury that dead bastard yourself. How's that sound?"

"That ain't a Christian way to talk."

"Might be I've lapsed."

I moved past my aunt, into the main room, just as eager to leave as I'd been the last time I was here.

Constance had moved in with us after my mother died. Supposedly it was so she could take care of my father and me, but I understood even in my youth that she'd run out of people willing to put up with her. My father was drunk most of the time, and Constance had the personality of a charging bull. She bellowed her way into the house not long after the last bit of dirt was settling on my mother's grave, and she never left.

Whatever individual failings my father and my aunt

possessed, they became something altogether worse living under the same roof. My father gave up on his life. Wanted nothing more than to be in the ground with my mother. And Constance did her best to put him there. She came in, claimed everything of my mother's that she wanted, and put the rest out to burn. My father paid no mind, just drank and worked up new complaints to hurl as often as he could, and Constance would snap back with a practiced sort of spite that had endured between them for a lifetime. They were like starving animals, pulling the same bit of meat from a bone, neither of them ever getting a big enough piece. Always hungry and always angry.

My mother's memory suffocated in that house.

Being there turned my stomach. The place still smelled like spilled whiskey and the dead, flowery stench of my aunt's perfume.

I wanted nothing more than to go home to Galveston and never come back.

"Just take them books if you mean to." Constance followed me out to the wagon, where I put the books into a small trunk that I'd brought along. "Don't know why I even sent for you. Did you a kindness, letting you know about your father."

"Let's go see the preacher." I knew arguing with my aunt was like feeding coal into a furnace. I started walking toward the church, taking a slightly faster pace than I figured she could manage, but she dogged my heels, digging at me about those books the whole way.

That woman was powered by pure meanness.

The preacher saw us coming and met us on the front porch of the church. I was starting to think nobody in this town wanted me to come inside.

He was the same old man who'd mumbled some words over my mother's grave and hurried us all out of the churchyard so he could get back to sneaking drinks from a bottle or judging people or whatever it was he did with his spare time. I couldn't remember his name, but Constance supplied it.

"Preacher Cuthbert, might be you remember my nephew, Floyd? He's come to pay for the funeral."

"You took your time coming," Cuthbert said. "This burying is overdue. And to tell it plain, your daddy is beginning to smell. Flowers can only cover up so much. Don't many want to come to church with a body smelling up the place. Your delay in arriving has put us at some inconvenience, young man."

I had not been young for some time, but Cuthbert was nothing short of ancient. His leaky eyes moved across me but never could seem to catch hold. Cuthbert appeared to be wearing the same faded gray wool suit from twenty years ago, but he'd shrunk inside it. He looked like a stick man someone had dressed and placed in front of the church to scare off sinners.

"Well, I got here as quick as the Lord allowed me, I guess."

Constance grunted. "My nephew has more disrespect than he can contain. It keeps spilling out, making a mess."

"I remember that quality about him," said Cuthbert.

A pair of children squatted in the shade beside the steps leading up into the church. A boy and a girl, they both paid close attention to the proceedings. Preacher Cuthbert stood at the top of the stairs, looking down at all of us like devils in the pit, Constance included, but it seemed her desire for conflict didn't extend to holy men.

I had the ten dollars ready, and I climbed halfway up the steps to hand it to him. "Ten dollars. Do you need anything else to proceed?"

Cuthbert counted the coins slowly, like he was certain I was trying to shortchange him. As he counted, the little girl chimed up and said, "I'm sorry your daddy died."

The preacher stopped counting and started hollering. "I told you children to scatter. Y'all find somewhere else to go. Nobody wants to come to church if they have to walk past a pair of orphans with their hands out."

"Or when the sanctuary smells like a dead man," said Constance, eager to throw her weight behind the preacher.

"Yes, as we've already established," he said.

"I appreciate your kindness," I said to the girl. "But it wasn't much of a loss, to tell the truth."

"See how he is," said Constance.

"Ten dollars even." Cuthbert pushed the money deep in his pocket. "That will cover the barbering, the coffin, and the burying. You want a little wooden cross with his name on it or something, that will be another ten dollars."

"I don't think that's necessary," I said.

"Well, ain't that a sad state of affairs?" said Constance.

"It don't surprise me a lick," Cuthbert said. "Young

people have lost all respect for the rest of us."

I walked back down the steps and stood beside the children. They looked healthy enough, but clearly hadn't had a bath in a while. The girl had blonde hair and a permanent grin on her face, like she knew things the rest of us didn't. The boy wore a heavy pistol on his belt and a look like he was chewing on something bitter. I couldn't help but notice that look was directed at the preacher, and I thought maybe Cuthbert might want to go inside before the kid figured out how to use that gun.

"Now that you're ten dollars richer, do you think you might find something for these kids to eat?"

Preacher Cuthbert looked at me like I'd suggested he embrace the devil and all his designs.

"These children are heathens," he said. "And the girl is at least twelve. That's old enough to work for your dinner."

"Is that true?" I grinned at the children. "Are you two heathens?"

The boy stood up to speak. "My mother used to call us that when we acted up, but I don't think she really meant it."

"What happened to your mother?" I asked.

"She burned up," the boy said. "And my daddy too. Preacher said that fire was the best way it could have happened, else he'd have had to charge us for a double burying."

His sister stood, brushed off some of the dust from her dress.

"My name is Nellie Abernathy," she said. "My brother's

name is Hank. We're pleased to meet you. What Hank means is, our house burned down with our parents inside. We were sleeping on the porch, otherwise we'd have gone with them."

"Might have been the stove caused it," said Hank.

"Might have been something else." Nellie gave a sidelong look at the preacher that suggested there was more to the story than she was willing to discuss here.

"I'm sorry to hear it," I said. "How long ago?"

"Almost four weeks at least," said Hank.

"Thirty-nine days," said Nellie.

"And every one of them days, here you sit on my steps with your hand out." Cuthbert slapped his palms together when he spoke, working himself into a froth. "I never saw these children or their parents attend services in this church once, but now they're expecting a warm welcome. Well, God knows what's truly in your heart."

"You'd better hope that's not true," said Nellie.

"See there," said Constance. "Talking to a preacher like that. Probably best their parents burned up before they could teach them any more of that blasphemy."

"You're a foul old woman," I said.

"And you're nothing but a heathen, just like them kids."

The horse and wagon waited for me back at the house and there was nothing to be gained from standing there any longer.

"Children, how about y'all come get something to eat?"

I started walking and they fell in line behind me.

Constance and Preacher Cuthbert shouted after us,

but they weren't saying anything worth listening to.

We reached the wagon, and I showed the children the store of food I'd brought along. Nellie fought the instinct to dive in like an animal, at odds with her own hunger, but Hank stuffed his mouth full of salt pork in a hurry, and with a little urging, Nellie offered her thanks and began to eat as well.

"Do you have any family nearby?" I asked.

"None that are still alive," Hank said.

"No one here that will take you in?"

"Nobody has yet," Nellie said.

I could see the church across the main square of town. Constance with her hands on her hips, the preacher with my ten dollars weighing down his pockets. Both of them staring a hole through us.

Men stopped feeding logs into the saw blade, took a water break, and watched. Others lingered in the shadows between buildings or peered out from beneath shredded canvas awnings. A group of feral-looking children perched on a pile of broken river rocks, soaking in the heat of the day like thirsty snakes.

Every one of them, watching Nellie and Hank eat.

My charity had gone against the fundamental darkness that held sway in Old Cypress, and I knew then that if I left them behind, Hank and Nellie would either die of neglect or grow into the broken sort of people surrounding us.

They had no belongings apart from their clothes.

"Children? Have either of you ever been to Galveston?"

The children rode cross-legged in the wagon as we headed south. The road traced the same path as the river for a way, and the black line of water appeared in the gaps between the trees. Mosquitoes swarmed, and the humidity was suffocating, even for someone accustomed to Galveston. The children kept quiet for at least two hours before Nellie's voice startled me from the lull of travel.

"Your house is near the ocean," she said.

"Close enough," I said. "A few blocks."

"Neither of us have ever seen the ocean."

"Well, give it a few days and that's going to change."

"The ocean's beautiful," she said.

"You've seen a picture of it?"

Hank spoke up. "No, she ain't. She's just using her whisper talk."

"Say again?" I said.

"Hank, be quiet," said Nellie.

Hank ignored his sister. "She's got whispers in her head that tell her things. Like they told her how we should be at that church this morning to make sure you found us. And you did, didn't you?"

"That's not how it is at all," Nellie said. "Not most of the time, anyway. Mostly, I see things and I feel how things are. It's hard to explain."

"And sometimes you hear words," said Hank.

"Rarely."

"Now you're just making up stories," I said.

"I don't tell lies, Mr. Betts," said Hank. "Nellie don't neither."

Taking the children with me had been a quick decision, but with enough time behind me to have given it some thought, I realized how ill-equipped I was to provide even the simplest guidance to them. I thought about Mrs. Elder and what she'd think when I came home with two orphans in tow. I felt confident she'd help me sort out a solution, but it embarrassed me that I'd need that sort of help. I was a master carpenter. I could build a house without help from anyone. But this whisper-talk nonsense was driving home the point that children were complex puzzles, not easily solved. I had no business being someone's guardian, and certainly not their father figure.

"We won't burden you, Mr. Betts," said Nellie.

"I never said you were a burden."

"I can tell you're a good man," she said. "You don't have to prove that to us. We're all of us orphans now, so I guess we can be that together. We're all going to be okay, at least mostly. I believe that much for sure."

"I'm glad you're optimistic," I said. "Me, I'm just hoping Mrs. Elder doesn't let my room to somebody else before we get back."

I knew better than that, and Nellie seemed to know it too. She laughed. "You'll always have a room at Mrs. Elder's house, I think."

"What do you know about it?"

"Nothing, I guess," she said.

"She knows more than she lets on," said Hank. "It's enough to frustrate a person sometimes."

"Choose to be kind," Nellie said. "Being spiteful does not become you."

With that, Nellie fell quiet.

We rode along for several miles, and all the while I could feel her ruminating. That sounds strange, but it was like something was pushing up behind me, scratching at my brain. I could feel Nellie riding in the wagon behind me, quiet as the grave, until the silence seemed to gain a life of its own. The creak of the wagon dulled. The river stopped chirping. The bugs grew still and retreated into the cool shadows. And when Nellie started speaking again, her words tumbled right into my brain.

"I know you're lonely for Mrs. Elder and might be she's the same way for you. I know you didn't like your father very much, but you miss your mother dearly. Every day. I can feel how much beautiful life there is in Galveston. I can see all the different paint colors on the houses, and the way the sun falls and squeezes in between them so that you have to look away or it hurts your eyes. I can feel lace tablecloths and wet sand and fresh-sawn lumber against my palms. And I know that life is about to get very hard, but that's nothing new."

"Jesus," I said.

"I can't tell you much about *him*." Nellie was out of my head now and speaking aloud.

"Where'd you get these books?"

I looked over my shoulder and Hank had the trunk open. He was flipping through a copy of *Herodotus* with narrowed eyes.

"Those were my mother's," I said. "We used to read them together."

"I love books," Nellie said.

"I like stories," Hank said. "Just not when they're in books."

"The best stories are in books," Nellie said.

Nellie dug into the trunk and soon enough she was reading out loud from *A Tale of Two Cities*. Hank seemed disinterested at first, but Nellie had read the book before, and when she explained to her brother that there would be people having their heads chopped off with a guillotine, he warmed up to the story. She was a smart child, rarely stumbling over the words, and her soft voice carried us along like a boat on a peaceful river. I was shaken by the power she had to get into my mind, and though by almost any measure it should have been frightening, it was evident there was no darkness in what she could do.

She paused in her narration from time to time to show Hank how to sound out words, to point out a tiny copperhead barely visible near the riverbank, to run her fingers through her brother's hair in a vain attempt to comb it down. Her conversation leapt from proper dental hygiene to George Washington to the right way for Hank to fold a handkerchief and stuff it in his shirt pocket, like she needed her brother to know everything under the sun and wasn't sure where to start. Whether or not she understood it herself, Nellie had taken over her dead mother's role.

After a few hours of this, Nellie stopped reading mid-sentence and snapped the book shut.

"Somebody is in trouble," she said. "Hank, be alert with your pistol in case it's needed."

"Hank, do not draw that pistol," I said.

Nellie was up on her knees in the wagon now, trying to look out ahead of us. What passed for a road cut through some low brush and ran close to the river again, but there was nothing ahead of us but miles of swampland.

"I'm an expert pistoleer," Hank said. "Don't worry about me, Mr. Betts."

"That doesn't matter. Keep it in the holster."

I didn't like the thought of Hank waving that pistol around, taking shots at shadows. He was just as liable to shoot me or one of the horses as whatever he was aiming at, and I was convinced the power in that pistol would put the boy on his behind if he pulled the trigger.

Nellie was close behind me now, and I could feel the worry leaking off her.

"Do you have a gun, Mr. Betts?" she asked.

"I have a rifle with me, in case we want to hunt some supper."

"Maybe you should take your rifle in hand."

"Nellie. Tell me what you're on about."

"We're about to encounter some scoundrels."

"Say again?"

"Some bad men," she said.

"My pistol's loaded, at least," said Hank.

The horses led the wagon around a bend, and we saw another wagon, pulled off the road in the trees near the river's edge. It was tall and enclosed, with wooden panels that would open up along the side, and the panels were bound shut by what looked like rusted baling wire. Professor Finn's Healing Spirits, Waters, and Mystical Tinctures was painted on the side in sloppy red letters. The wagon looked uncared for. Planks of wood had pulled away in several places, revealing the wagon's dark interior, and the metal tire on one of the wheels was warped. I could envision that tired old wagon moving down the road like a man with a limp, rattling whatever questionable wares were stored inside, and shaking her passengers down to their bones.

A pair of sorry horses pulled the thing, their ribs like saw blades on the underside of their skin. They lapped at the river and swatted at mosquitoes with their tails.

Two men—one of them, presumably, Professor Finn—wrestled with something at the water's edge. They looked to have captured a giant fish, or maybe an alligator, and bound it in ropes, but were having trouble getting the monster out of the water and up the riverbank. The fish thrashed and fought in the shallows as the men struggled against it.

"They're hurting him!" Nellie said.

"They're just fishing," I said. "Caught a monster, looks like."

"He's not a fish," said Nellie. "Look at him."

"He's got a face!" said Hank.

"Maybe an alligator," I said.

"He's a person," Nellie said. "They're going to kill him."

Nellie climbed over the side of the wagon and ran toward the commotion.

"Get back here!" I said.

"She ain't listening," Hank said.

I set the wagon brake, climbed out, and followed her.

Nellie was engaged in a full-throated rebuke of the two men by the time I caught up with her. They had managed to get the fish onto shore, and the larger of the two, a giant who was a foot taller than me and had to weigh over three hundred pounds, squatted on top of it in an effort to keep it still, while the second man tightened the ropes around their catch.

"Put him back!" she yelled. "Let him go. He's not an animal."

"Quiet yourself, girl," said the man with the ropes.

He wore a long, cowhide coat that was far too much for the weather, and a bowler hat that clung tight to his head, no matter how hard he struggled against the fish. He was clean-shaven but for sideburns that grew to sharp points, and a pair of wire-rimmed glasses with one lens missing rested far out on the bridge of his nose. Sweat poured down his face, and he gritted his teeth as he cinched up the last knot binding the still-thrashing fish. He stepped back, clapped his hands in satisfaction, and turned to face us.

"You're making a terrible racket," he said to Nellie.

"Let him go, scoundrels!" said Nellie.

"I'll do no such thing. And it's no business of yours."

"Nellie, come on!" I said.

"Yes, Nellie," said the man. "Listen to your father."

"It's not a fish." Nellie looked up at me, tears in her eyes. "These scoundrels are going to harm him."

"You keep calling us scoundrels like you just learned the word," said the man in the bowler. "Perhaps you need to broaden your vocabulary."

"I have an extensive vocabulary," said Nellie. "I call you that because it's the name that best suits you."

"You're an insolent thing. If my daughter was speaking to someone that way, I'd lay a palm up against her face."

"You do that, you'll find yourself short one hand," I said.

The man grinned like he was trying to eat something dead and convince you it tasted good.

"Forgive my manners," he said. "You came upon us during our struggle with this monster of the sea, and my blood is still running hot. I'm Professor Finn. You may have heard of me?"

"I have not," I said.

"Surprising, if you've spent any time in these parts."

"I spend as little time as I can in these parts."

"Well, that explains it. My medicines and curiosities are well-known. People are positively delighted to see this wagon roll into their town. Toys for the children. Healing balms for grandmother's aches. Special concoctions for would-be lovers. Arthritis and tuberculosis and fevers, all cured thanks to me. And of course, a few oddities from the four corners of the earth, to entice the thrill seekers. Things that can be experienced nowhere else. Have you any interest in seeing a genuine jackalope skull?"

"I can't say that would appeal to me."

"You're not a professor," said Nellie, "and he's not a fish."

"Young lady, I assure you I studied at many of the top schools in the eastern part of this great continent. Schools where only the finest gentlemen are admitted. Places of quiet reflection, where the yammering of hard-headed children is forbidden. You are correct, however, that this is not a fish. This is one of the wonders of the world. My companion and I have been following stories for years. Chasing down false paths. I was not even entirely convinced of his true existence until I laid eyes on the monster myself, but as you can see, he is real. Imagine what someone might pay to see such a creature, and I'm letting you look for free."

I finally looked at the struggling fish.

And, of course, it was no fish. It was a man, covered in scales as I've already described him. And when he stared at me, blinked, and bleated like a sheep, I felt my legs nearly buckle underneath me.

"He doesn't belong to you," Nellie said.

"What the hell is it?" I asked.

"He does in fact belong to me," Professor Finn said. "You have just witnessed the beast's capture. How can you question it?"

Having been bound tight, the creature had given up most of its fight. It lay there, bleating. I'd never heard anything more sad or miserable, and when it peered up at me again, I had to look away.

The giant who'd been seated on the fish stood. A fat-bladed knife as long as my forearm hung in a scabbard on his hip. I remembered Nellie's unheeded warning to have my rifle at the ready.

He wore a white shirt, stained from a thousand dinners, and suspenders with tarnished brass buckles. His pants stopped just below his knees, and he was barefoot. Either he'd lost his shoes in the river mud while he was fighting the fish creature, or he just went around barefooted. A bloated beard hid most of his face, save for a flat nose that looked to have been broken more than once, and eyes that looked right through you. The hair on his head fell in long, greasy strands, like the seaweed that washed up on the beach at home.

Professor Finn held out a hand toward the giant with a flourish, as if introducing the next act in a traveling circus. "My associate, Kentucky Jim."

"Y'all ain't taking this fish," said Kentucky Jim.

"Nobody said we were taking anything," I said.

Nellie continued shouting. I could feel the wobbly sensation of her mind being put to special use, and I recognized she was using her whisper talk.

"Nobody is happy to see you come to town, but they're happy to be shut of you when you leave. I have a better word for you than scoundrel. It's charlatan. You're a thief. Stealing people's money and selling them lies. I think maybe you believe half the stories you tell people at this point. Your friend, at least, is an honest liar. He doesn't buy his own tall tales. And this fish man is not going to star in any traveling freak show, so you can get that out of your head. He is not an animal. He's likely a better person than you are."

"I suggest you control your daughter, sir," the professor said.

Nellie stood close enough to Professor Finn that he could have reached out and grabbed her.

"She's not my daughter," I said. "But we're leaving."

I tried to grab Nellie's arm, but she shook me off.

"You believe my whisper talk?" she asked me.

"I guess I might. But we need to leave these men to their business."

"Their business is binding the fish man in chains and parading him around to be mocked. They'll beat him for fun. Starve him. That big one there is wondering what it would be like to cut off a little piece, a finger maybe, just to see what color his blood is."

The professor grunted, and you could see the mask of civility slowly falling away from his face. "My friend can do anything he wants to this beast because he belongs to us. Go back to your wagon and leave, or we may find out what things he wants to do to you."

Nellie bolted around Kentucky Jim and began fumbling at one of the knots binding the fish man. Jim grabbed her with no effort at all and tossed her into the river.

Well, hell.

I came after Jim, knowing the outcome in advance, but

left with no other options. I aimed my fist at his chin as he turned back to face me, but the blow glanced off him and he put me down with a punch that felt like a house collapsing around me.

On my knees in the river mud, I saw the fish man staring me in the eye. Understanding. Intelligence. Not an animal.

A kick, like a shotgun blast to my midsection, and I was down all the way. On my back in the mud with the fish man, the sounds of Nellie's screaming, desperate to pull me back from the growing darkness. I remembered the promise of Jim's big knife, and I waited for it.

Then a gunshot sounded and locked us all in place.

Nellie was on top of the fish man, trying to untie him. Kentucky Jim loomed over me, knife in hand. The professor was at his side, like he was keenly interested to learn what my insides looked like. Make a study of them.

And when I turned my head and looked up the riverbank toward my wagon, I saw Hank with that heavy Peacemaker in his hand, aimed right at us.

His grip was steady.

"You shot the wagon spoke!" Professor Finn said. "Busted it in half."

"Where do you want the next one?" Hank asked.

"Put that pistol down, son," the professor said. "Elsewise we're going to have to kill your daddy."

"My daddy's already dead."

Hank pulled the trigger again and the bullet went through Kentucky Jim's wrist. He howled and dropped his knife. It stuck in the mud just beside my head.

I sat up, trying to shake off the dizziness. Jim and Professor Finn scrambled away, hiding behind their wagon so Hank didn't have a clear shot at them. I pulled the knife from the mud and began sawing through the fish man's ropes.

"He doesn't belong to you!" yelled Professor Finn.

"Might be you can repair one wheel, but two would be a real chore." Hank shot again, and another wagon-wheel spoke splintered.

"Now that's enough of that!" Professor Finn peeked around the edge of the wagon, and I wondered if he might have a gun hidden under his long coat.

"My brother is a crack shot." Nellie worked to free the fish man as I kept sawing on his ropes. Her grin was so wide I wondered if maybe she'd lost her mind. "I suggest you stay hidden back there until we're far away. If you give him something to shoot at, he won't miss."

"You're going to die for this, little girl," said Kentucky Jim.

"You should listen to him," said Finn. "Continue with this folly and you'll have forged mortal enemies. This is our livelihood that you're interfering with. Leave now and this will be forgotten."

"None of us will soon forget this." Hank shot again and clipped the yoke between the two horses. They started and jerked the wagon forward. They splashed into the river, pulling until the wagon became wedged in the mud. The Professor and Kentucky Jim scampered to keep the wagon between themselves and the boy. They were like water moccasins, seething in the river.

We finally freed the fish man from the ropes, and he stood, angry and dripping with muddy river water. I backed away, afraid of what the creature might do now that he was loose, but Nellie grabbed one of his webbed hands with both of hers and shook it, drawing his gaze down in her direction. She smiled, and I could feel that scratchy feeling of Nellie using her whisper talk. Something passed between them, and then the fish man nodded and allowed Nellie to lead him toward our wagon.

"Come along," she said. "We've overstayed our welcome here. Hank, keep that pistol pointed at those two charlatans until we're out of sight."

"You don't have to tell me that." Hank took another shot, and it splashed in the water near Professor Finn's wagon.

"You shoot my horses and you'll be in worse trouble than you are now!" said Professor Finn.

"I wouldn't shoot no horse," said Hank. "You come out from hiding and I'll put one through your neck, though."

Nellie climbed into the back of our wagon and invited the fish man to follow.

I hurried to catch up with them. "Nellie, we can't take him with us."

"We most certainly can."

The fish man hauled himself up into the wagon and squatted next to Nellie, chest heaving. Hank sat beside them, that heavy pistol held steady in the direction of

Professor Finn and Kentucky Jim.

Nellie hollered at the pair of them. "You two stay right where you are until we're a long way from here. And if we see you in Galveston, my brother won't have any problem resuming his target practice."

The fish man started up with that wet bleating sound and I figured we'd best get far away before he decided to take some revenge on his captors.

I climbed up, took the reins, and hurried the horses back onto the road.

The children peppered the fish man with questions, and he continued bleating as if doing his best to answer. Within a few miles, Nellie had determined that he was a long way from home, and that he was in favor of traveling with us all the way to Galveston. Might be the ocean was where he came from originally, but Nellie explained again how the whisper talk wasn't an exact science.

Nellie also learned his name, but she said it was not a name that our mouths could pronounce, so she asked the fish man permission to call him Charlie after a cat she'd had that was eaten by an alligator.

Charlie agreed that was fine with him.

NELLIE

The way I saw it, I'd made two terrible mistakes.

First was playing tricks with Mr. O'Casey's imagination. Why did it matter what kind of dark thoughts were occupying his hateful mind; my family and I would have soon been beyond his reach. But I hadn't been able to help myself. I had to give him a bit of the pain he'd wished on others, and I'd been wrong to do it. My mother knew how I'd behaved, of course, read my guilt like a book. But even in her dying moments, she'd done everything she could to absolve me. She peered right inside my soul with a forceful command to never blame myself for what was happening. It wasn't my fault and nothing I could have done differently would have changed my parents' fate.

But how we wish to feel about something, and how we *actually* feel about it, are two entirely different things.

My second terrible mistake was mentioning to the two scoundrels what our destination was. Galveston, by the sea. It didn't occur to me until after nightfall, when we were already long gone from the scene of the altercation. Mr. Betts was eager to distance us from the pair of snake oil salesmen, and he drove the wagon like hell was coming up behind. The horses were tired, and so were we, but he kept us going deep into the night. When he finally reined up to make camp, Charlie and Hank were asleep in the wagon and I watched him tend to the horses with heavy eyelids.

"I think those men will come after us," I said.

"We have enough head start. I doubt they'll find us."

"Mr. Betts, I'm afraid I made a mistake."

"How's that?"

"I lost my temper, taunting those men. I believe I told them we were traveling to Galveston."

"I don't think you said anything about it."

"I'm pretty sure I did."

The encounter at the river had been chaotic, and I couldn't recall everything I'd said, but I was almost certain I'd mentioned Galveston. Regardless, we would need to operate with the expectation we were being followed.

"It's alright, Nellie. They'll have to figure out how to fix that wagon or else ride those sad horses, and either way they'll be slow moving."

"But they'll catch up," I said.

"Might be they will."

"Then I'll rouse Hank and make sure he reloads his gun."

"Let Hank sleep," he said. "We won't need any more of

his talents tonight. How'd he come to be so skilled with that pistol?"

"Father taught him," I said. "He wasn't that good of a shot himself, but Hank took to it fast. I've never seen anybody outshoot him."

"Your father was a good man?"

"Yes," I said. "I believe he was."

Mr. Betts nodded, staked the horses to the ground. He moved like a man who ached in his muscles and his mind. Slow, deliberate, making sure every task was just so before he moved on to the next. Most people guarded their thoughts, if only from themselves. They tried to squash every awful thing they were thinking down into some dark corner, so they could believe in a better version of who they were. I understood more than most that it was easier to fool yourself than it was to fool others. But not Mr. Betts. He was layered with sadness and a bit broken by the world, but he owned who he was, and clung to a sort of uneasy peace within his soul that kept him moving forward.

When Mr. Betts asked about my father, a gray flash escaped his mind, the image of a drunken man hollering from a doorway as his son rode away. And over that dark scene, a wash of golden light across the sky, which I understood to be Mr. Betts's vision of his mother, mourning from above.

"Your father teach *you* anything?" he asked.

"Some things, I suppose," I said. "But I learned more from my mother."

Whether I'd accidentally put the thought in his head, or Mr. Betts was simply perceptive, he looked over at me and grinned.

"You mean to say your whisper talk?"

"Yes, that and more. But it's less like she taught it to me, and more like she taught me how to deal with it. She was afflicted with the whisper talk too. It's something in our blood."

"Afflicted?" he said. "You see it as something bad."

"I honestly don't know," I said. "Some days, yes."

Mr. Betts finished his tasks, sat down beside me on the ground. We hadn't bothered with building a fire. The night was hot enough, and there was no reason to call attention to ourselves if we were indeed being followed.

We were both coated in dried river mud, and I couldn't decide which one of us smelled worse. I'd been wearing the same dress for more than a month. Mrs. Partridge, who taught school in Old Cypress, had snuck us some old clothes that her children had outgrown, despite the prevailing sentiment against helping us. That was as much as she was willing to risk for charity, but I was grateful we hadn't spent all this time in our sleep clothes. Mr. Betts wore wool pants and a green button-up shirt that were in far better shape than the clothes Hank and I were wearing, but he'd been traveling in the wagon for nearing two weeks, and we were both in desperate need of a bath.

Mr. Betts ran a hand through his lanky hair, worry coming off him in waves.

"I'm sorry about what happened," he said, "but I'm

glad they were good to you. I'm glad you and the boy have good memories. I believe you were well loved."

The way he said it with such certainty, I was sure I'd shared some of those memories without even meaning to.

My dress had a small pocket sewn into the side. I reached in, took out the three nails we had blessed the night my parent died. Hank and I had visited the ruins of our home nearly every day since it burned. The stone hearth and chimney remained intact, an accusatory finger pointed at the sky, and it was surrounded by a piled-up nest of charred wood and blackened memories. On one of our visits, I climbed into the destruction and dug through the ashes until I found those nails, undamaged and ice cold. I had no idea if they still contained any power, or if they ever had, but once I had them in my possession there was no putting them back.

Mr. Betts saw me rolling the nails over in my palms.

"What do you have there?" he asked.

"Some pieces from our house," I said. "Some nails."

Omitting the true nature of the nails seemed like a betrayal, but no matter how good a man I believed Mr. Betts to be, he wasn't ready for the whole truth. My whisper talk worried him enough. If I started talking about spells and witches, it would fundamentally change the way he saw me.

Besides, maybe they really were just nails.

They were cold; they were lifeless.

And as far as I could tell, they hadn't done much to keep our home safe.

"I'll make sure the two of you are taken care of, somehow," said Mr. Betts.

"I know."

"I won't allow you to be mistreated again."

"I know that too."

"Your whisper talk tell you that?" Mr. Betts smiled at me when he asked the question, but I knew he wanted an answer.

"A little bit," I said. "But your actions tell me more than anything I could draw from your mind."

Mother had taught me not to rely on the whisper talk alone when forming opinions of people. What went on in the mind did not always translate into action. Some people seethe with hatred and jealousy and all manner of petty emotion, like Preacher Cuthbert, but they don't understand that about themselves. They carry on like they're the pinnacle of virtue. And there are those like Mr. O'Casey who know exactly what kind of awfulness they contain within them, but refuse to admit it, even in their own dreams.

Whisper talk made one thing plain—people rarely understood the truth about themselves.

Everyone has dark thoughts, selfish notions they're ashamed of. But the only thing that really matters is how they handle themselves in the living world.

I hated being able to understand people better than they understood themselves.

"I don't have many secrets," said Mr. Betts. "I guess I'm not the interesting sort."

"It's nice," I said. "You're kind to help us."

Mr. Betts wasn't uninteresting, he was just sad, and that sadness overwhelmed everything else he was feeling. He had a hard family life, I could tell that much, and whether he understood it or not, he was eager to help Hank and me replace the family we'd lost. Eager to help Charlie get home. Mr. Betts would be helping himself, in a way.

"Your whisper talk is not a bad thing," he said.

"You don't know anything about it."

"That's true, but you have a way of connecting with people that most others can't. The way you figured out right away what kind of men we were dealing with at the river. The way you make me feel like everything's going to be okay, when I should be doing that for you. And the way you bonded with the fish man."

"With Charlie," I said.

"Yeah, Charlie."

"I don't really believe everything is going to be okay," I said. "The truth is, I don't know."

"Nobody knows," he said. "So, you aren't any different than the rest of us, Nellie. We just figure it out as we go along and hope for the best."

I clutched the nails so hard in my hand that they stabbed into my palm, and tears streaked down my face.

Memories of my mother's screams echoed in my head, and I could see a black wall of water, roaring like an invading army across Texas, washing away everything I ever loved, and all the people that might love me back.

There was a life to be had for me beyond all this, a new family to be forged, but there was also a chance that every one of us would drown beneath that surge of violence.

Everything would *not* be alright. I could feel it.

But we all had to face what was coming anyway.

The road that cut through the thicket was sloppy and rutted, and it took us three days to escape the pines. Beyond the trees we encountered more wide-open space than Hank and I had ever seen, and one glance along that endless horizon made me dizzy, like I was being pulled someplace I wasn't sure I wanted to go. Yellowed grass grew as high as the horses' flanks and rippled like the surface of a slow-moving river. The sun hung white hot and angry overhead, and while the breeze cut the heat a little, we rode through long stretches without any trees to offer shade.

We eventually reached a place called Beaumont. Mr. Betts stopped the wagon outside the town proper and announced he had business to attend to. He meant to get a few quick supplies, and to cable ahead to Mrs. Elder that he would not be returning home alone. Charlie would attract attention, so he had to stay in the wagon, and Mr. Betts asked Hank and me to keep an eye on him. Like either of us could keep Charlie out of trouble if he set his mind to it. But Mr. Betts was willing to leave us alone with him, and that said a lot about how comfortable we'd all become with Charlie in such a short time.

Charlie had a *way* about him. None of us believed for a second that he was dangerous.

Before heading into town, Mr. Betts rolled Charlie a cigarette. I didn't approve of smoking, but it was evident that Charlie was familiar with the habit, and he was an insistent sort. He had a way of pinching the cigarette in his webbed hand and holding it up to his mouth. He'd inhale, make a grunting sound, and release all that smoke back out his gills.

"Can I try it?" Hank reached out to Charlie, like he expected him to pass the cigarette along.

"You most certainly may not," I said.

"But Father used to let me, sometimes," said Hank. "When nobody else was around."

"That doesn't mean it's a good idea."

"Charlie Fish don't care," said Hank. "Do you?"

Charlie sat quietly, choking out smoke like a locomotive. He seemed to know better than to get between the two of us on the matter.

"Don't call him a fish," I said.

"His name's Charlie and he's a fish, so his whole name should be Charlie Fish."

"He's not a fish."

"He's close enough," said Hank.

Charlie bleated, and I felt acceptance blow through my mind like a cool breeze. Charlie didn't care what we called him, and he was letting me know. Ice ran up my back, and though I'd become accustomed to conversations with Charlie, it still left me unsettled sometimes.

It was the same way people felt about me.

I'd spent the last couple of days working to figure out Charlie, to find out what kind of man he was. And make no mistake, he was a man. Maybe not a man like Father or Mr. Betts, but he wasn't any sort of animal. He appeared to understand everything we said, and I took that to mean he'd been away from his home and at least in the vicinity of humans for a very long time. That also explained the smoking and the way he pitched in to help Mr. Betts prepare meals and to drive the wagon. But the more I'd poked at Charlie's mind, the more he'd reached into mine, and I realized that he hadn't just latched on to my whisper talk in some way. He had a talent of his own. Not whisper talk exactly, but close enough.

Neither of us were normal. We existed outside the understanding of human reason.

Charlie and I might as well have been kin.

Hank sat with his pistol in his lap, like he expected bandits to ride down on us at any moment, but his attention was fixed on Charlie. Hank reached out, ran a hand up and down Charlie's arm, feeling at his shimmery scales.

"Stop petting him," I said. "He's not a dog."

"I'm not petting him. He just feels funny."

Hank kept on grabbing at Charlie. Feeling the spines that ran up his back. Poking him in the ribs to see if he was squishy. Charlie made no move to stop him. He endured Hanks's examination with good humor and smoked his cigarette until there was nothing left but ash.

"Wish I could have gone into town," said Hank.

"I do too."

"The men who caught Charlie might be there," he said. "Maybe they passed us. If I was there, I could help protect Mr. Betts."

I smiled. "We need you here to protect *us*."

"I guess you're right," he said. "But I'd still like to see the town at least."

"I can show you."

Hank nodded, understood what I meant.

We were close to town. Close enough that I could feel the mental energy of several thousand people. It was hard for me to imagine a place so big, but when I opened my mind to the clamor, Beaumont became real to me. The hiss of steam and the clang of metal on metal. Railroad lines threading together in complicated knots. Train cars stacked up one behind another, filled with East Coast finery, pigs headed to market, passengers with lives that extended far beyond the boundaries of this part of Texas that I'd always called home. I could smell wet cattle in the streets and hear men grunting back and forth at one another, tossing heavy bags onto wagons at the rice mill. I could taste whiskey and feel chewing tobacco lodged between my lips and my teeth. I watched farmers lead oxen, their faces burned red by too much sun. Children swam in the river and flatbed boats floated nearby, overloaded with lumber.

When I first met Mr. Betts, I'd seen glimpses of Galveston. Scraps of memory and emotion that gave me a pretty picture of his home, and how Mr. Betts felt about it. But there were so many unguarded thoughts here, so many visions of Beaumont, that I might as well have been walking the streets beside him.

I opened up, showed Hank all of it.

But I held back the things I couldn't understand. A black sea, buried deep in the earth, ready to break loose and explode into the sky. And again, the images of raging water, the ocean falling on us like a collapsing mountain, washing away everything in its path. This time, though, I saw faces in the water. Not human, but blue-and-green-gilled people, just like Charlie, swimming against the torrent. Mewling like cats in the tempest. Calling him home. At least that's what it felt like.

"Charlie," I said. "Is that your family?"

Charlie's thoughts poured into mine, moved with the ferocity of that coming storm. I understood he meant well, but this time there was no nuance to Charlie's version of whisper talk. It felt like he was squeezing my head between his massive hands, and it started to hurt. All those faces from the water spoke at once, but I couldn't understand what they were saying. The storm crashed down around me; I felt like I was standing beneath a waterfall.

The voices grew louder, more insistent.

"It's okay, Charlie," I said, pushing back. "Just tell us what you want us to know."

The pressure relented, and I could feel something like shame coming from Charlie.

Hank was breathing like he'd run a mile, and I knew Charlie was showing him things too.

Colors flowed through my field of vision. Shades of blue and green and gold that I'd never seen. They followed underwater currents that pulled all of us along in their wake; they ushered us deep into the ocean, through gardens of sea plants swarming with fish, and beyond the rocky escarpment that marked the edge of the shallows. We plummeted to unexplored depths. The water smelled like flowers and unfamiliar spices. I shouldn't have been able to smell anything, shouldn't have been able to breathe, but we were inside Charlie's mind now, and this was his world to reveal. We cut through ancient canyons furred with golden plants and crowded with mottled seashells. We raced past skinny sharks and schools of swordfish, silver and bright as the moon. We passed over a range of undersea mountains, like birds in flight, and we plunged, through a pass in those mountains, into the mouth of a cave, and finally slowed inside the belly of a massive cavern, lit bright as high noon by green moss that clung tight to every surface.

Within the cavern was a city. It was unlike any I'd ever imagined, but Charlie made me understand where we'd traveled.

This was his home. Coral structures that resembled tall buildings grew from the ground, from the walls, from the roof of the cavern. There was no up in this city, no down. Just *inside*. Like every structure was another tooth in a giant, gaping mouth. And hundreds of beings like Charlie, maybe thousands of them, hurried about their business just as the people in Beaumont did, unaware that we drifted among them like ghosts, unseen but taking an interest in their lives.

They cut through the water quick as alligators. Quick as catfish cut loose from the line.

Charlie's home was beautiful.

Two of the underwater people floated toward us, not moving on their own, but caught up in the current. Despite the green light coming from all directions, their faces were hidden in murky darkness. They drifted closer, still as stones. It wasn't until they were within arm's reach that I saw their faces and realized they were my parents. Mother with her long blonde hair floating upward from her head, and Father right beside her, gripping her hand in his. They were blue and dead. Eyes wide open but empty. I made to scream, but water rushed into my lungs, salty and cold.

It was like I'd breathed in sadness.

It overwhelmed me. My parents floated there, close enough to touch, and there was nothing I could do to bring them back.

Charlie was beside me then. He put a heavy arm around my shoulders and gave me a hug. And I realized these weren't my parents. How could I have mistaken them? They were beings like Charlie, still floating, still glassy eyed and dead. But not my parents. Understanding calmed me. I realized that Charlie was just trying, in his curious way, to explain that his parents had died here. That the loss had chased him away. I don't know what happened, but *something* had happened, and he'd run away from home like a terrified child. Maybe he *had* been a child, afraid and unsure how to go on living without his parents, or eager to distance himself from his own memories. I understood that. Maybe Charlie had gone looking for another home, but never found one as good as the one he left.

It was obvious he wanted to go back there.

How many years had he been gone? How many decades?

Charlie wailed, and the sound rumbled through the water like a thunderclap. The undersea people noticed us, turned our way all at once like they were a single living organism. Connected. Family. They circled around us in a flurry, faces pressed in close and crying, gills flexing in and out, bubbles rising, wide black eyes questioning. Charlie wailed again, and they all joined him to form the mother of all storms, a roaring answer to whatever Charlie had begged them for. And their reply washed us away, sent us flying up and out of the ocean like waves against the beach.

I opened my eyes. Gasped for air, as if I'd really been submerged. The sun was high in the sky, and it burned away the last of the images Charlie had shown us. Hank and I were back in the wagon. The afternoon air was thick, and we were all covered in sweat. Charlie had his arms around both of us, hugging us close. I could feel his gratitude, though for what, I wasn't yet sure.

I could also feel the sadness coming off him. Sadness for himself, and sadness for us. Like he understood exactly what had happened to Hank and me, or what *would* happen to us. I didn't want to know which. And I couldn't figure out why he'd shown us his home. I'd been asking him to tell us about himself for days. Maybe he figured out he could trust us, or maybe he finally saw us as kindred souls who shared the same sort of loss.

I wasn't sure, but I thought maybe it had more to do with my whisper talk.

Charlie Fish hugged me tighter and showed me I was right. His memories came to me soft and quiet this time, like pages of a book being slowly turned. He'd run away from home, so long ago that even he couldn't remember how many years it had been. It hadn't taken him long to realize his mistake, but once he'd backtracked through the rivers and swamps he'd escaped to, he'd been unable to find his way back to his cavern.

He'd called out to his people, so many times, begging them to come guide him home, but they never heard him.

But now, with my talents added to his?

"Did they hear us?" I asked. "Are they coming to get you?"

Charlie bleated, filled my head with the image of a beach, waves slipping up the sand and pulling back again, taking Charlie with them.

Taking Charlie home.

"Whole lot of orphans in this world," I said.

Charlie bleated again, and Hank started to cry.

When Mr. Betts got back from town, we were all eager to press on to Galveston. None of us foundlings were certain what waited for us there, but whatever it might be, there was no turning back now.

FLOYD

THE MORNING AFTER we arrived in Galveston, I left the children and Charlie with Mrs. Elder and walked downtown.

The heat was alive and stalking the streets. My hat band and my shirt were both wet with sweat after just a few blocks. It was that point in September when you could begin to imagine what it would feel like when fall rolled in and the heat finally relented, but it was only a dream. We had a good month yet, maybe longer, before the summer heat would vanish.

My plan was to find Mr. Jansen and get hired back on with his building crew so I could start paying my rent again. There was always employment to be had for carpenters in Galveston, and I was confident I could be working by midmorning and earn at least a half-day's wage.

But first I'd decided a discussion with the police would be advisable.

The police station was quiet, even for so early on a

Friday morning. In the back corner of the room, four officers gathered around a square top table, playing dominoes, and they didn't look up from their game even when the Gulf wind slammed the door behind me. Another officer sat behind a metal desk near the entrance scribbling something down in the book with a pencil nub. He glanced up when I entered, looking mildly put off at the interruption.

"Help you, sir?" The officer had red hair, clipped short, and he wore his mustache so long that I could barely make out his mouth moving when he spoke.

"Might be you can," I said. "Officer?"

"Shelby. Sergeant Shelby, if you will."

"Sergeant Shelby, what are you hearing about the weather?"

One of the domino players hollered from the back as he was giving the tiles a shake. "It ain't no hurricane so don't let nobody tell you otherwise."

Shelby shook his head and chewed at the end of his pencil. "The boys at the weather service put the flag up last night. Best I can tell, it's going to blow pretty hard, but not liable to be more than we're used to around here. Are you a local, or just here to visit the beach?"

"Yes, sir, I live here. Floyd Betts. Pleased to meet you."

"You just come in for a weather report, Mr. Betts?"

"Well, no. I wanted to warn you there are some hard characters might be coming into town. A couple of old boys I met along the road some miles north of here. I believe they're criminal types."

"They're hunting after you?" he said.

"I can't say with any certainty," I said. "But we had a difficult encounter, and they don't seem the sort to forget a slight."

"And what is it you did to draw their ire?"

Shelby flipped to a new page in his book and started making notes, and I realized I wasn't sure what I could tell him. *Officer Shelby, we stole a river monster from a couple of snake oil salesmen. They attacked us and I fought the villains off with the help of a plucky schoolgirl and a nine-year-old gunslinger?*

None of that would do.

Shelby eyed me with practiced skepticism, and I realized I was clutching my hat a little too tight in my hands.

"I wasn't the instigator," I said. "These two men attacked an orphan girl I was traveling with, and we had to fight to get away from them."

"Where'd you come by an orphan girl?" he asked.

I explained the reason for my trip to Old Cypress and the circumstances that had landed Nellie and Hank in my care.

"Taking on them kids was right charitable of you."

"Wasn't no other good choice to make," I said.

"Others might have made a different one."

"I might have too, on my worse days."

Shelby's face pulled together in what might have been a smile. The tension around his eyes relaxed, and he licked the end of his pencil and asked me for a description. I told him all I could about Professor Finn and Kentucky Jim, excepting the parts about how they'd hunted and captured Charlie Fish. And I made the judicious decision to leave out the bits about Hank and his skill with a sidearm.

One of the domino players spoke up again. "The man calls himself Kentucky Jim?"

"Yes."

"Sounds like something a gambler would call himself. Maybe Mr. Betts here got in a tangle with the man over some money."

Shelby sighed. "Go back to your game, Harold. Quit with the undue speculation."

Harold shook his finger at Shelby. "I'm just saying, you can't be sure who the criminals are here."

"Harold," said Shelby. "Enough."

"Alright, then."

Sergeant Shelby turned back to me, sweat beading his brow and exasperation plain in his eyes. "Harold ain't entirely wrong. I'm not saying I don't believe you, but I can't go around arresting strangers on your good word, you understand. No offense, I don't know you any more than I know them. So, who's to say which party's in the right?

"Tell you what I'll do. I'll keep a watch out for these men you described, and if I see them, I'll question them about their actions. That's all I can do unless they commit some sort of crime here. Is that satisfactory?"

"Yes, sir," I said. "That's all I'm asking."

Shelby closed his book to signal our business done.

"Have a good day then," he said. "And tie anything

down you don't want blowing away. Tonight's going to be windy."

"Ain't no hurricane, though," said Harold.

I thanked them and left, wondering if I'd gained anything from the visit apart from a small measure of embarrassment and a questionable weather report.

I found Mr. Jansen, and by midday, he had me up on a ladder, hanging clapboard siding on a house at the edge of downtown. Wind gusted in from the Gulf, rattling windows in their panes and tossing sawn-off bits of lumber through the streets like gambling dice. Seagulls perched on swaying power lines and along the eaves. The air smelled of salt and sweat and hot blowing sand. And for the first time since I'd ridden out for Old Cypress, I felt like I was in full control of my circumstances. The simple rise and fall of my hammer. The dull, not unpleasant burn as I worked the muscles in my forearms. Conversation and laughter from the other men on the job mingled with creaks and moans and hissing exhalations of steamships laboring in the bay. I gave little thought to roadside criminals, or to what raising a pair of orphans might entail, and when the westering sun drew close to the horizon, I was sorry for the workday to end.

I climbed down the ladder, my shirt soaked with sweat.

Even on the ground, the wind whipped and tugged, and I considered possibly stopping by the weather service on the way home to get an unfiltered view on matters.

A hand gripped my shoulder and a familiar voice spoke. "Mr. Betts. We meet again."

I recoiled from the hand and turned to see Professor Finn and Kentucky Jim, a pair of storm clouds, blown into town.

"Have we startled you, sir?" asked Professor Finn.

He was dirty from the road, caked in dried river mud, but still carried himself with the air of an aristocrat. His hat fell slightly askew, and he gave a slight bow when he spoke again.

"We are not here to trouble you, Mr. Betts. Please don't think it."

"You just being here is trouble, I think."

Finn grinned as if I hadn't insulted him. Kentucky Jim hovered behind him, big enough to block the wind. He'd wound a dirty cloth around his wrist where Hank had shot him, and it was black with blood, like the wound wasn't healing right. He was pale and sweaty, and looked like he wanted to gut me right there. The rest of Mr. Jansen's crew loaded up tools, traded jokes, and drank heavily from a wooden water barrel. Others peeled off in search of something harder to drink. I knew I'd best find a way to slip away from Finn and Kentucky Jim before the other workers left. Else they'd have me alone and that wouldn't end well.

"Trouble, or opportunity?" said Finn. "That choice belongs to you. My companion and I talked it through on the way here. Had some time to mull things over. Now, we aren't normally the types to forgive those who've wronged us, you understand. No, sir. The type of slight you've delivered; well, we generally pursue those with a deadly sort of doggedness. But we realized, it wasn't exactly you who started all that trouble. It was that little girl, wasn't it? And her little scrap of a brother was the one that engaged in all the shooting. I believe you may have been thrust into circumstances beyond your control. A reluctant participant in their larceny, if you will. Have I taken the true measure of the situation, or am I mistaken?"

"The children and me acted in good conscience," I said, "and I won't distance myself from our actions."

"A little distance might be good for your health," said Kentucky Jim.

"How'd you find me?" I asked.

"This is a big city," said Finn, "but not so big. And full of friendly types. A person can ask around and learn a great deal. Who exactly was it you rented this buckboard to, mister liveryman? Floyd Betts, you say? And where might I find him? Why, he's my cousin, and we haven't seen each other since we were a pair of sprouts playing at war games with wooden pistols. Lives in a Mrs. Elder's boarding house, you say? Hires on sometimes with Mr. Jansen's crew. Well, I can't wait to surprise him. Here's hoping he even recognizes me."

"I won't let you hurt those children," I said.

"Neither one of us would think of it," said Finn.

I doubted that. Kentucky Jim looked like he was thinking on it a lot.

"We have a proposition for you," said Finn. "You have no need for the man fish. And those kids are likely more of a burden than you can handle. I understand they don't really belong to you?"

"Don't you ever stop talking?"

Finn patted me on the arm, like we were pals. "I'll admit I'm a talker. Came by it honestly. My mother could talk a salesman into his grave. Here's the thing, though. I learned love and compassion from that sainted woman too. And that's what brings me here today. Our design is not to harm the children. Far from it. We intend to make them a good life."

"They'll be fine without you."

"Listen to me, Mr. Betts. I didn't come bearing threats or idle talk. I came loaded with cash money to resolve our differences." Professor Finn reached for his inside jacket pocket and removed a stack of ten-dollar bank notes, counted out five, and fanned them in front of my face. "I have here fifty dollars, American. Now let me tell you how our transaction will work. You will take this money, and it will buy us back our newest star attraction. You stole the beast, so I'd say us paying you for him is more than fair. This money will also buy us the children. The girl seems to have a way with the man fish, and we may need her steady hand to keep him in line. And that boy, well he appears to be a crack shot. A shootist of the highest order. Jim here can attest to that. Now our traveling show is already quite popular, but if we were to add a man fish and a trick shooter, well we'd be moving up in the world. Might even leave behind all the backwoods towns and take our review out west. That sort of spectacle would draw crowds even in San Francisco. There is money to be made, so I am willing to pay you to make this easy, even though you have really done nothing to earn it. You cannot turn down found money."

"You might be surprised," I said.

"Mr. Betts, I don't mean to be indelicate, but you don't seem all that well to do."

"I get by."

"You get by on your own. But I can't imagine you're in a position to care for those children. Financially, I mean."

"I'll just have to work harder, I guess."

They both pressed closer, but I managed to keep from flinching. Finn still held the money up, like fifty dollars was enough to buy my soul. I didn't want to think about how such men came by their money, and I knew that if I were foolish enough to accept it, they'd kill me and take it back as soon as they had Charlie Fish and the children in hand.

"There is another option," said Finn. "One where you don't get any money and we take what we want anyway. Paying you is easier, cleaner, but we are comfortable with the hard way when circumstances demand it. You can tuck this money under your pillow and dream of all the things it will buy you, or you can wash up on the beach with your neck snapped. You decide. But do it quickly. It's too hot out here to linger."

"There it is," I said. "The monster that hides beneath the still water. You can't keep him under for long, can you?"

"I don't take your meaning, sir."

"I mean you like to put on like you're educated and civilized, but in truth, you're a low man, cut through with a violent streak. Is my meaning clear now?"

"Might be you're right, Mr. Betts. In which case, do you think it's wise to test me any further?"

"You can keep your money," I said. "And if I see you come near any of us, I'll let Hank take a few more shots at you."

"A poor decision. We'll not trouble you anymore this evening, sir. But we shall certainly come calling again soon." Finn smiled, backed away, and pulled Kentucky Jim along with him. Mr. Jansen approached with his wallet open, eager to pay me and get home to his supper, and he either didn't notice the men slinking away from his construction site or didn't recognize them as a threat. Kentucky Jim kept glancing back at us, as if figuring on whether or not he could kill both of us on the spot and get away with it. I talked with Mr. Jansen for a second, feeling the whole time like my heart might escape my chest, and when I looked up again, Professor Finn and Kentucky Jim had vanished into the loud bustle of Galveston.

The sun pitched farther to the west and shadows spilled through the streets like some angry god had overturned an inkwell.

My first instinct was to go straightaway to the police station and enlist Sergeant Shelby's aid, but Finn wouldn't have a hard time finding out where Mrs. Elder's house was. He might know already. Might, in fact, be headed there now.

I pocketed my pay and ran all the way home.

The four of them were gathered in the parlor when I arrived. Mrs. Elder served a cup of evening tea to Charlie Fish, who appeared engaged in a mental conversation with Nellie. Charlie was pressed tight into a wingback chair, his webbed hands gripping the wooden armrests like he might fall out. Nellie stood beside him, one hand on his arm, their eyes locked. Hank slouched on Mrs. Elder's overstuffed divan, reading a dime novel about Buffalo Bill. When I hurried into the room, I interrupted this scene of domestic bliss, and they all turned to me with varying degrees of exasperation on their faces.

Hank clutched the book to his chest. "Mrs. Elder said you wouldn't mind if I borrowed this one to read. I found it in your room. You don't mind, do you?"

"No, I don't mind."

"I can only make out some of the words," he said. "Nellie has been helping me, though."

"That's how you learn," said Nellie. "Keep reading. Mother always said persistence will be rewarded."

"I believe we have a problem," I said.

"You're a mess, Mr. Betts," said Nellie.

"Mr. Betts has been working," said Mrs. Elder.

Charlie Fish bleated and Nellie laughed.

"Did you know that Buffalo Bill once performed for the Queen of England?" Hank held up the book as if I hadn't seen it before. Cowboys and Indians capered in a circle around an illustration of Buffalo Bill and his long mustache.

"Of course he knows," said Nellie. "That's his book you're reading."

"Well maybe he ain't read it all."

"What you mean to say is maybe he *hasn't* read it all," said Nellie.

"I think I could shoot good enough to join up with his show. Do you think so, Mr. Betts? You've seen me shoot."

"Listen here," I said. "Those scoundrels tracked us down."

Nellie's word for them—scoundrels—had taken root in my brain and I could think of them in no other terms. Nellie and Charlie Fish both turned to face me, the two of them moving together like they were of one mind. Nellie's laughter was gone, and she shook her head back and forth slowly as she spoke.

"Well, this is all my fault then, isn't it? I'm the one who told them where to find us and now they have."

"This is in no way your fault," I said. "They're bad men and you can't account for what they'll do."

"You've seen the men in Galveston?" asked Mrs. Elder.

"Yes, and spoken with them."

"They haven't harmed you?"

"No," I said. "But I'm sure they'd have liked to."

Mrs. Elder crossed to the front door and locked it with her key.

"You children, please close the windows and make sure they're all locked. And Nellie, if you would, ask Mr. Fish to kindly keep watch on you while I find something for Mr. Betts to eat."

"Yes, ma'am."

Mrs. Elder led me to the kitchen and directed me to a seat at the small dining table in the corner. She gathered remnants of the evening meal while I told her about my trip to the police station and my encounter with Professor Finn and Kentucky Jim. I sipped self-consciously at a cup of tea, realizing how bad I needed a bath, and how miserable I was for having brought all of this trouble to her doorstep. Eventually, she settled in across the table with her own cup of tea, and we sat together in companionable silence for a few minutes while she considered everything that had happened.

"Well, I won't put those children out, and I won't leave Charlie to fend for himself either," she said.

"We're of the same mind."

"I know we are, else I'd have put you out in the street already." She smiled when she spoke, but I knew she meant what she said.

"I'm sorry for all this."

"It's no more your fault than it is Nellie's."

"No matter, I'm still feeling the blame."

"Do you think it would accomplish anything for me to visit that Sergeant Shelby with you in the morning so we could swear out a warrant together?"

"I doubt it. You haven't even seen the scoundrels yet, and anyway, the police didn't seem inclined to do much to help unless I presented evidence of a crime."

Mrs. Elder chuckled. "Scoundrels."

"It's what Nellie calls them."

"Still, it's funny."

"She's an interesting child," I said.

"Interesting falls a little short in describing her."

"Precocious, maybe?"

"You're getting closer," she said. "I spent a lot of time with them all today. I learned a whole lot more about your Charlie Fish."

"He's *my* Charlie Fish now?"

"No, I don't believe he belongs to anyone," she said. "Nellie says he's originally from the ocean, not from whatever creek you pulled him out of. She says his family is coming to get him too."

"His family?"

"Yes. He's been gone a long time, but now he's back and his family is coming to take him home. Meaning back to the deeps, I suppose."

"So, there's more like him?" I asked.

"According to Nellie, yes."

"She say when they're coming to get him?"

"I don't think Charlie gave her a schedule," she said.

"Mrs. Elder, I think it might be better for me to take Charlie and the children and find somewhere else to hide. It's plain to me that both the men coming for us are killers. Ain't no telling about Charlie's family. We can't assume they're all as obliging and housebroke as he is, can we? Trouble seems attracted to me. I don't want any more of it latching on to you."

"Have I ever given you the impression that I'm a soft flower in need of your care?" she asked.

"No, I was only. . ."

"I grew up hard, Mr. Betts. If you think my life has been nothing but sewing and afternoon tea, you're mistaken." Mrs. Elder returned her teacup sharply to its saucer, stared me down with a ferocity I'd never seen from her. "I've been underestimated more times than I care to remember. By my family. By a whole lot of men, including Mr. Elder. All of them thinking they had a better idea than I did about the way I should live my life. They were wrong, and you're wrong. I won't have you selling me short."

"That's not my intention."

"To hell with intentions. I don't run away from hard times. You can leave if you like, but Charlie and the children are staying here with me."

"If you want us here, we'll stay."

"Yes, you will."

"Okay."

"I don't think you'd be able to convince Charlie to go anywhere with you anyway," she said. "He's eager for his family reunion."

"Well, at least someone around here has some kin they can brag about."

Mrs. Elder allowed herself a tired grin, but her eyes still burned with nervous energy, and whether she wanted to admit it or not, a little bit of fear. She reached across the table, took my hands in hers, left them there without offering a reason. Something turned over deep inside me, and I wished again that we might be able to figure some things out between us.

"Mrs. Elder. Have I ever made it clear how fond I am of you?"

"Not with your words," she said, "but no time for all that right now."

"Never seems to be time."

"No, there never does."

"You're risking your life to help these children. To help me. I don't know what I can do to properly thank you."

"What you can do is you can quit calling me Mrs. Elder. Start calling me Abigail."

"I'd like that," I said. "And you can call me Floyd."

Abigail smiled. "Oh, I think I'll keep with Mr. Betts for now."

NELLIE

Mrs. Elder wouldn't admit she was frightened, but she spent the evening fretting about the house, wiping down dishes she'd already scrubbed clean, and making sure the new clothes she'd bought for Hank and me hung in the wardrobe straight as arrows in a quiver. She worried at a stain on her tablecloth that had likely been there before she'd inherited it. And every time she passed a window, she parted the curtains with her fingertips and peered outside, just in case those scoundrels might be lurking in the mist.

Mr. Betts was exhausted from his labors, so he got a basin of water and a cloth, cleaned the sweat and grime from his face, and retired to bed just after dinner. Hank followed not long after, yawning and swearing to anyone who'd listen that he wasn't remotely tired. Charlie followed Mr. Betts to bed, but we heard him clomping around upstairs for a while longer, and I suspected he was watching out the windows too, though I'm not sure if he was looking out for Professor Finn and Kentucky Jim, or for his brothers and sisters and cousins to come marching out of the water and up the beach.

The door was locked and the windows shut tight, so the heat of the day remained trapped inside. That didn't deter Mrs. Elder from her tea. From what I could tell, the woman drank it morning, noon, and night. Having double-checked the locks, she sat a kettle and an extra cup on a serving tray, then placed the tray down on the squat cherrywood table located alongside her divan. Mrs. Elder then heaved into her wingback chair with a half-defeated sigh. She'd tried to usher me along to bed with everyone else, but I had no intention of sleeping until I grew too tired to resist. I was still convinced that my foolishness had summoned the scoundrels here, and lack of sleep was only a fraction of the penance I deserved.

Mrs. Elder sipped her chamomile, pointed at the tray on the end table between us. "If you insist on staying up with me, at least have some tea."

"No, thank you," I said.

"Tea will help you stay awake."

"I'm not sleepy."

"Neither was Hank." Mrs. Elder grinned when she spoke, and I knew she was pulling my leg.

"Hank didn't put everyone he knows in peril."

"Neither did you," she said.

I wasn't raised to argue with adults, so I didn't respond. Mrs. Elder leaned over to the window, peeked out again. The night was so quiet I could hear the heartbeat of the ocean, steady against the beach.

"Nellie, I'll keep watch," she said. "I don't believe they're coming tonight. Might not be coming at all."

"I'll probably know they're coming before you will."

Mrs. Elder considered this, finally gave in. "I suppose you might be right about that, if all you told me today is true."

"It is."

"I believe you," she said.

And she did. I could tell it.

We'd had a pleasant afternoon getting to know one another. Mrs. Elder had questioned me first about Charlie, of course. He was more interesting than Hank and me by a wide margin. But once I'd explained all I knew about Charlie, she'd naturally been curious to know how I figured out so much.

I'd been taught not to tell anyone outside the family about my whisper talk, had kept it a sworn secret since my days of toddling around the yard in baby shoes. But I'd offered up the truth to Mrs. Elder just as quickly as I had to Mr. Betts, and I hoped it was the whisper talk itself guiding me, giving assurance that these weren't the sort of people I'd grown up around. These people could be trusted.

If I was wrong, it was too late anyway.

Having already reckoned with a fish man having a smoke in her parlor, Mrs. Elder had little trouble believing in my whisper talk.

As with Mr. Betts, though, I'd held some things back.

I sat on the divan, hands in my lap, flattening my skirts. I kept casting my thoughts out beyond the walls of the house, like a fisherman's net, hoping to catch the scoundrels arriving before they could surprise us. But there were just *so many* people. Opening my mind like that was an invitation to chaos. I quickly realized there was no way I could single out Finn and Jim until they came close enough to strangle me. And besides, even the collective thoughts of the whole population of Galveston couldn't compete against the slow, lumbering approach of the storm that I could no longer deny.

Every minute ticked closer to whatever was coming. I hadn't sorted out exactly how bad things would be—whisper talk doesn't measure things out precisely—but in the quiet evening with so little to distract me, the dread was like a heavy quilt, swaddled up tight around my body. It put me in mind of what happened to my mother. Killed, along with her husband, just because of her magic. The same kind of magic I had. And I was certain that whether I was swallowed up by the ocean or stuck in the chest with Kentucky Jim's eager blade, I would not meet my death from old age. Maybe the guidance I gleaned from whisper talk was a blessing, but I was more convinced than ever that the power running through my blood was a curse.

And whatever hope I had of learning about it, of controlling it and doing some good in the world, had died with my mother.

I'd never be able to master it without a teacher.

Soft rain began to strike the roof, and I realized my hands were shaking.

Mrs. Elder leaned forward in her chair, took hold of my hand in hers. "Have you always been so anxious?"

"No, but circumstances have conspired to make me so."

I started to cry. For more than a month, I'd dedicated myself to keeping Hank and me alive. Scrounging for food. Avoiding the sort of people in Old Cypress who might decide it was better for the two of us to follow our parents to whatever hell awaits witches in the afterlife. Simple survival had overtaken everything else, and there'd been scant time to mourn. All the willpower I'd used to keep those feelings at bay vanished in the comfortable gloom of Mrs. Elder's parlor, and all the misery of the last month broke free.

Mrs. Elder moved over to the divan and put her arms around me. I cried until there was nothing left. Then I told her everything about me. Even the things I hadn't shared with Mr. Betts. I explained about Mother and her witchcraft; all the things she'd promised to teach me that had been burned to ash. I talked about the sometimes-terrible nature of the whisper talk and how it could come upon you like a creeper from the shadows, whether you wanted it to or not. And I showed her the three nails, which I still carried with me all the time, and explained how my mother had poured all her magic into those unremarkable pieces of iron, trying to keep us safe. How I'd helped with the spell, and how it had failed. I was afraid Mrs. Elder would blame me for all the terrible things I'd brought on my family, and all the danger that followed me around like a stray dog.

But instead, she just listened. And when I'd cried myself out, I felt lighter. Like Mrs. Elder had taken some of my sadness and drawn it into herself.

"You've endured more than your share of awfulness," said Mrs. Elder.

"And there's more coming," I said.

"We'll manage," she said. "You seem more resilient than any of us."

"I don't want to be resilient," I said. "I just want things to be normal. I want *me* to be normal."

"I know something about not being normal, young lady."

"You have some sort of magic too?" I said.

"Oh, heavens no," she said. "Nothing like that. But my upbringing was unconventional. Probably even more than yours."

"I can't imagine that," I said.

Mrs. Elder put a hand on my knee, leaned close, and lowered her voice like we were conspirators in some grand plot. "We're just telling stories amongst ourselves here, right? No need to share all this with the others?"

"Of course not," I said.

"I come from a family of criminals."

I couldn't help but smile. I'd have been less skeptical if she'd told me she was from a family of elephants. The best way I could describe Mrs. Elder was *put together*.

She kept her boarding house just so. Her linens were without wrinkles. Her ceilings were entirely free from cobwebs. Her floors shone like the noonday sun. She kept her life on a schedule like a train conductor. Mrs. Elder was a bit older than my mother, more mannered and in control of her world. She was pretty and sharp-witted, and with her tea and unerring good humor, the furthest thing from a criminal I could imagine.

If there was a wildness to her, it was buried so deep underneath her good manners that even my whisper talk hadn't uncovered it.

"You don't behave like a criminal, Mrs. Elder."

"I didn't say I was a criminal. I said my people were all criminals."

"What kind of criminals?" I asked.

"Rascals. Horse thieves. Worse."

"Tell me."

Before she even began to speak, I saw dull-brown images of a man with a patchy black beard, flailing and screaming as other men pulled him from a stone shack, like they were dragging a monster from its dark cave out into the cleansing light. They bound the monster in ropes. I could feel the rasp of those ropes around my wrists. I could feel a hempen noose cutting into my neck.

"My father fought in the War Between the States," said Mrs. Elder. "Left to fight not a month after I was born, and me the youngest of six. The rest all boys. So, you can imagine how my mother struggled during those years. Well, when Father returned, he was different. He'd grown harder. Figured out he was good at killing. And my brothers had become half-wild in the intervening years. This is all what I was told, mind you. I hardly recall my father at all. He was hanged as a killer when I was six."

The noose drew tighter, and tears welled in my eyes.

"Are you okay, Nellie?"

"Yes, ma'am," I said. "Please keep going."

"Father was finished with honest work at that point. I don't know what all he did to keep us fed in those days, but I know what got him hanged. He walked into a saloon in San Antonio, proceeded to get drunk on nickel whiskey. And there were some men there, engaged in a high-stakes card game. Father decided he was bold enough to rob them. Well, it's easy to wave your gun at gamblers like that when they aren't expecting it, but not so easy to evade pursuit when they come looking for you. My brother June told me later that our father came away from that gambling table with near three hundred dollars. And he was able to enjoy it for all of three days before they found him and dragged him away."

"They hanged him from a live oak branch," I said.

Mrs. Elder leaned back, gave me a look like she was still trying to figure me out. I could feel her thoughts grow more guarded. She wanted to share, but she wanted to do it on her terms. After a few seconds she stood, started double-checking the locks. Peeking out the windows again. Like if she busied herself, the painful story would be easier to distance from.

"That's exactly what they did. At least, that's what

June told me. He'd have tried to stop them, but there were five or six armed men. Too many. Father visited that saloon all the time. Wasn't even a stranger, so I don't know how he expected to get away and not be found. I don't think he was a smart man. But he fancied himself an outlaw. No surprise to me how he ended up."

"I'm sorry to hear it," I said.

"Sorry doesn't factor into any of this," she said. "I appreciate the sentiment, but you and I both know sorry never changes anything."

The walls in the house groaned, like the air outside had become heavy. The rain picked up, rattled hard against the windowpanes.

"Mother didn't last long after all that," she said.

"She died?" I asked.

"No, she left. Had her fill of us, I guess. We woke up one morning, and she'd packed a few things and ridden away on the blue roan we called Betsy. Never saw Mother or that horse again."

The horse was beautiful, and so was the woman in her saddle. Long, curly hair and eyes that caught the rising sun in such a way they looked like silver stars. She was rope thin and anger had chipped her away to nothing but sharp angles. The version of her mother that Mrs. Elder shared with me was soaked in sadness and regret, and she rode low in her saddle, keeping her head down like she was afraid to look either of us in the eye.

"Sometimes all we want is to be in control of our own lives, and we do whatever it takes to make it so," she said.

"Whether that's right or wrong, it's the truth all the same."

I considered what I might do to gain some control over my life. I doubted I'd leave everything I loved behind, but even though the whisper talk granted me a glimpse into a possible future, I had no way to predict how it would affect me, how I'd react. Might be I'd make the same choice as Mrs. Elder's mother, if my trials continued down the path they followed now. I wondered how much misery I could hold inside me before my personality began to change, before I became a person who chose being alone.

Maybe even a person who chose death.

"My brothers took care of me in their way," said Mrs. Elder. "At least they didn't turn me out to fend for myself."

Mrs. Elder's five older brothers were eager but broken. You could tell by the looks in their eyes, by their predatory grins. They were boys in need of guidance. Boys let loose to run wild on the world, who knew no other way than to live on the underside of society. My mind overran with images of midnight escapes on stolen horses and back-alley attacks against unwary gentlemen. Saloon brawls and broken bones. Gunpoint robberies and drunken celebrations. And weaving through it all, a little girl with red hair, who could only be Mrs. Elder, mending her brothers' clothes and cooking their food, and occasionally, standing watch while one of the boys broke into a barn, a house, a general store. I could hear breaking glass and splintering wood, and the memories smelled like whiskey, sweat, and stolen cattle.

"They all became criminals," she said. "And I helped them. Sometimes. But I do not consider myself a criminal. I was a child, and what else could I do but go along with them? They were older. They were my brothers. We don't get to choose our family or our raising."

I wanted to tell her I was sorry, but we'd already established there was no point.

"Eventually, they married me off."

"You found a husband?"

"They found me a husband," she said. "June had a friend in Galveston who owned a few stores here in town. This house we're in belonged to him. A man named Tobias Elder. And Tobias was good friends with the mayor at that time. June was in a fix for robbing a brothel off The Strand at gunpoint, and half the lawmen along the coast were hunting for him. He didn't have a lot to bargain with other than a pretty sister, so when I was fifteen, I moved to Galveston and married Tobias. June left town with his arrest warrant canceled, and, I suspect, a pocket full of money. It worked out well for both of them, until it didn't. That's the last I saw of my brothers, but I heard years later that June was shot in the face by a Texas Ranger. He always aspired to robbing banks, and finally worked his way up to it, I guess. He wasn't any smarter than my father was.

"I was never happy with the arrangement, you understand. I did not want to be married to anyone, least of all a man I'd never met. But I never knew anything other than doing what I was told and figuring out how to survive from one day to the next. I was a good wife to Tobias because I figured that's what was expected of me. I look back now and realize I should have ridden away one night, just like my mother did. But I never wanted to be like her, even if I did have a better reason for leaving. No one was keeping me there but me.

"We were well off, which was something I wasn't accustomed to. Three meals a day. Society engagements. Clean clothes and this comfortable house. But Tobias had been given most of his businesses by his father, and they began to fail, one by one. That had nothing to do with me, except he liked to turn his anger my direction. He'd rarely been violent before that. Eventually, his behavior became . . . untenable. I warned him in plain terms to reconsider his treatment of me. He declined to change, so I sent him away."

"What do you mean?" I asked.

She gave me a look that suggested I knew exactly what she meant, but she had no intentions of spelling it out.

And she was right, of course. I could see it all, even the parts I had no desire to see.

"He was here having his fried fish dinner one evening, and the next morning he was gone. I won't say more about that other than the police were satisfied that he'd fled town to avoid debts, and after a few days of knocking on doors, they made no further inquiries."

"You've lived here since then?" I asked.

"Yes. I sold his businesses to pay off all he owed and turned this place into a boarding house. Life has been mostly pleasant ever since."

Tobias Elder lingered in Mrs. Elder's thoughts, but he was no more than a massive shadow. Hovering over her life, but insubstantial. Mrs. Elder had done her best to forget his face, to forget the gravelly sound of his voice, and so those things remained only as faint impressions. Nothing I could latch on to, no way to get a better picture of the man who'd once occupied the wingback chair every evening, reading his newspaper and sipping his whiskey. I cast about the room for any signs that he'd ever lived there, but nothing remained. No muddy boots by the door. No ashtrays clogged with cigar butts or brass spittoons by the hearth. All these things had been present once, but now the house was thoroughly Mrs. Elder's. It was as if she'd banished every memory of her husband and remade this place into the home she'd always wanted.

Mrs. Elder peeked through the front curtains one last time, then sat again in the wingback chair. Grasped the arms of the chair with both hands, and settled in.

There was no mistaking, the seat belonged to her.

"Listen, Nellie," she said. "I'm telling you all this to say we aren't required to live the story that's expected. Our lives belong to us. We need only decide what we want from life and then do our best to make it happen. If you want to follow your mother's path and learn about your magic, I'll do everything I can to help you do that. And if you decide you want a different life entirely, you have a home here until you figure out what that is. And Hank does too."

"And Mr. Betts?"

"Yes, him too," she said. "I don't know that I could shake him loose at this point."

"Mr. Betts is sweet on you," I said. "He's just shy about it."

"I don't need your magic to tell me that. Men aren't all that challenging to figure out."

"Do you think you two might get married?" I asked.

"I have no plans to marry anyone," she said. "And I'm too tired to think on all that tonight. Sometimes I just want to let life play out, without trying to predict every rise and fall. Even you don't know what's going to happen for certain. Am I right about that?"

"Yes."

"Good. I'd hate to think you have no surprises to look forward to."

"Knowing what's coming can help you prepare," I said.

"Yes, and knowing what's coming can also cause you to despair about things that can't be helped. Don't let the worry overtake you, girl."

She was right, but that didn't make forgetting my fears any easier.

The rain continued to come down, like heavy rocks striking the roof.

In my worried mind, that rain never stopped. It came down from the sky in buckets, filled the street and invited the ocean to leap across the beach and swallow every house on the island. It became so deep that the boarding house was entirely submerged. We could look out the windows and see the faces of Charlie's brothers and sisters, pressed up against the glass, bubbles rising from their gills. Their eyes were black and without emotion. The scoundrels floated off in the distance, dead and chewed on by sharks. All the residents of Mrs. Elder's boarding house huddled in the lantern-lit parlor, hugging one another close, until the ocean began to press, to squeeze. Until the sea people clung to every surface of the house, tearing, pulling, ripping. And then the boarding house came apart. The black sea swallowed the light and carried us all away.

A storm was coming for certain. But none of us, not even me, knew exactly how terrible it would be.

Eventually, Mrs. Elder fell asleep right there in her wingback chair, just put her head forward and closed her eyes.

I stayed awake all night. Listening. And when the wind began to throttle the house, just before dawn, I feared this would be our last peaceful sunrise.

FLOYD

NEXT MORNING, the ocean called Charlie to the shore.

A slow, steady rain had resumed overnight, and it ran off the brim of my hat in silver streams as I stood with Charlie, my boots sinking into the muddy beach. The clouds hung low over Galveston, compressing the summer heat against the buildings and the brick streets so that I felt like a biscuit in a Dutch oven in spite of the downpour. This summer had been hotter than most, and the rain settled into my clothes, warm as bathwater. The beach was crowded with tourists in bathing outfits, more of them than I would have expected with the weather. Breakers crashed against the sand, the bath houses, and the elevated trolly trestles with more violence than was customary, but the tourists laughed and clapped and scampered in the storm swells. There was an electrified excitement about them, like the threatening storm was a dark curiosity. A band of children had fashioned a raft out of old boards, and they bobbed and laughed, always on the verge of being toppled. All of this while furious rows of gray clouds crawled in from the Gulf, and the rain grew steadily harder.

I very much wanted to be back indoors.

Nellie had wrapped Charlie in one of Mrs. Elder's bed quilts and tied it around him with a sash. She'd pulled it over his head like a cowl, and the crowd was so enamored with the sea that no one had yet paid him much notice. We stood together, the waves pushing up to our knees. Charlie studied the horizon, searching. The ocean was black and boiling, like a huge pot of crawfish over a raging fire.

Not for the first time, I wondered if the incoming storm was going to be worse than everyone was expecting.

I had plenty of reasons apart from the weather to stay safely indoors, but Charlie had woken up intent on visiting the beach, and even Nellie couldn't sway his course. His wailing had been urgent. Nellie said she thought his family was getting close. Professor Finn and Kentucky Jim hadn't shown themselves during the night, but that didn't mean they weren't lingering somewhere nearby. I had no desire to accompany Charlie to the beach but I couldn't let him go alone, and all of us pitching in together wouldn't have been able to stop him.

A selfish part of me hoped he'd walk into the ocean and never look back. Maybe if Charlie was gone, our pursuers would cut their losses, leave us alone. Maybe I'd have a chance to figure things out with Abigail and the children.

Another part of me envied Charlie. He was planted

like a statue, quilt flapping around him, waiting for his people. He wasn't human, but he wasn't hard to read. Longing soaked him to the bone. I had to go way back in my memory to find any relatives who I'd be so desperate to reconnect with. Nothing pleased me more than to think of my mother, reading Nathaniel Hawthorne stories to me in front of the fireplace back in Old Cypress. I could feel her hand on my shoulder and smell the lye soap she used to clean our clothes like I was still sitting there beside her. But of course, she was long gone. I had a few fleeting memories of my grandparents back in Tennessee. Images mostly. Their smiles and the two of them, sitting on the porch steps, calling me into their arms. We'd left there when I was three and they were surely dead by now, but I could still call to mind the chickens in their yard and the old cat who terrorized mice in their barn. I'd go back to those times if there was any way, and I figured that was close to how Charlie was feeling. We'd likely never know how he came to be in that East Texas creek, but I imagine he endured his own hardships. His own version of life with a drunken father and with old Aunt Constance, ruining anything that was good.

We stood there near an hour, and I was desperate to get back to the boarding house. I grabbed Charlie's arm, felt the muscles like bridge cables beneath his scaled skin.

"Charlie, let's get back. What say? We can come again when it stops raining."

Charlie wasn't moving.

I thought about leaving him to head to the house, but I was afraid of what might happen to him if someone suddenly recognized what he was.

So, we remained there as the gray skies darkened and heavy waves throttled the fat support posts that elevated Murdoch's bathhouse twelve feet above the sand. The wooden structure spanned half a city block, running parallel to the shoreline. Wind shredded the American flag that clung desperately to a swaying pole mounted on the peaked roof. People gathered along the oceanside rails on Murdoch's long deck, safely above the swells, clutching umbrellas and lifting up children so they could better see the waters churn. It was just nearing eleven o'clock, but the storm had chased the sun into hiding. Electric lights were strung along the beach from pole to pole, and the dim, yellow bulbs jerked around like agitated fireflies in the growing darkness. A few vendors had set up tents and cook tables to sell fried shrimp, hushpuppies, and cold drinks, but the tents became canvas sails, carried off into the streets of Galveston, and the onrush of water grabbed hold of everything else and pulled it greedily back to the sea.

The swells rushed up the beach, advancing more than they were retreating, and I had to hurry back in order to keep from being claimed by the undertow. Charlie stayed where he was, the water coming nearly to his chest, back down to his knees, and then hammering him again.

I called out, but he wouldn't come.

Wouldn't be moved.

Bits of siding pulled away from Murdoch's, became airborne. Water hammered into a wooden changing station, about ten yards up the beach. Reduced it to broken boards and splinters.

"Charlie!"

The water raged, and Charlie bobbed in the surf.

Many of those who'd gathered at the beach scattered back to the street. The smart ones had already found someplace indoors to shelter. But others still lingered near the waves as they battered the shore. Lightning broke across the sky like cracks in an old silver mirror. The air was humming, and the earth rumbled. The violence of the storm burrowed into my bones, made me feel small. Rain kept pace with the wind, coming down in a torrent, gave the impression that everything people had built here could be broken into bits and disappeared from memory. We could all vanish tomorrow, and the ocean would continue to feed.

I tried holding my hat to my head, but finally gave up. It spun away, and I didn't bother trying to chase it. Whether I had to leave Charlie or not, I needed to get back to the house. Help Abigail nail the shutters closed. What was coming might be a hurricane and it might not, but it was already becoming dangerous, and deciding what to call it wouldn't make it any less fierce. I hollered for Charlie, but I doubted he could hear me over the crushing sound of the rain. I made up my mind to leave him when he suddenly turned, began fighting back against the waves. He tore free from the deepest water and ran toward me, mouth wide and bleating. He went past me like I wasn't there. His sodden quilt fell away, hit the water, and got caught up in the flow. I turned and chased after him, realized he was headed back to Mrs. Elder's in a hurry.

Charlie kept screaming. Something was wrong.

We hurried the two blocks back to the boarding house. The swells had pushed past the beach and water ran down the street, nearly ankle-deep. Mrs. Elder's house stood on five-foot posts, and it would take a mighty storm indeed to pass her threshold. But the flow of water outpaced us as we splashed toward home, and the wind felt like it might carry us both away.

Mrs. Elder was standing on the porch when we arrived, a rusty rifle in her hand. Rain flattened her, revealed her sharpness. Her long hair was undone and stuck to the sides of her face, and she hurried down the stairs to meet us with a wildness in her eyes that I'd never seen.

"Abigail?"

"They took the children," she said.

Charlie wailed, but he'd already known. I figured that much. Nothing was going to break him loose from the ocean's spell except maybe for Nellie. She'd sent out a distress call, and Charlie had answered.

They were tight, those two.

Up close, I could see a slow red trickle of blood running from Mrs. Elder's left temple. It was hard to tell how bad she'd been hurt because the rain washed away the blood as fast as it could flow.

"You're bleeding," I said. "Come here, let me look."

"No time for that. We need to find the children. They can't have been gone more than a couple of minutes. Your scoundrels busted in the door and the big one hit me before I could slow them down. Knocked me out of sorts for a bit."

"You're hurt," I said.

"I'm perfectly fine."

"Stay here," I said. "We'll go after them."

"You won't go without me."

"Abigail."

"Let's go."

Already Charlie Fish was splashing up the street in the direction of downtown, presumably following whatever mental breadcrumbs Nellie was leaving behind. Abigail fell in behind and I hurried to catch up.

"Where did you get that rifle?" I asked.

"Mr. Elder left it behind when he departed."

"Why'd they take the children?" I had to holler to be heard above the rain torrent.

"I don't know, Floyd," she said. "Probably figured we'd be willing to swap the kids for Charlie. I can't guess at motives for such men. I just intend to shoot them if I get the chance."

My hands felt empty, and I wondered if Hank had his pistol with him. I doubted it, else he'd have shot both of his captors before they could make it through the door, shot them both again before they knew the first bullets were in their chests.

Mrs. Elder proceeded unafraid, and I felt the guilt welling up inside me, knowing I was the one who'd brought all this trouble her way. Everything had accelerated so fast. A week ago, I was content to keep my mouth closed, to swallow down all my feelings. Now I wanted to beg her to go back to the house and take cover. Tell her I wasn't entirely sure how I'd live if anything bad happened. But words would never move her. I had placed us all in this predicament, and now we had to resolve it head on. Else our eyes would never meet again without seeing the failure in one another.

We followed Charlie Fish across the island, back toward downtown, toward The Strand. He never stopped to question his path, so I assumed that Nellie was calling out to him. I tried to think through what Finn and Jim might do, where they might go. If they only wanted the children, they'd be headed for the train, which crossed an elevated trestle back to the mainland, or to the ferry we'd ridden just the day before yesterday. But I didn't think they'd leave without Charlie. Abigail was right. The children weren't their prize. They knew the children would draw us to them, and they'd be waiting for us.

Rainwater pooled as we crossed the middle of the island, though it wasn't flowing through the streets like it was closer to the shore. Palm trees bowed along Broadway; leaves pulled loose and took flight like birds stirred from their nest. The wind circled around us, blowing from the ocean and the bayside all at once. I could taste sea salt in the air. Tiny frogs hopped from the street to the grass, hundreds of them driven into a frenzy by the rain. A fat, black snake cut through the ankle-deep water like a shark on the hunt, and I shooed it away with the side of my boot.

By the time we reached downtown, the usually calm bay waters were swelling into The Strand. The sidewalks had been built a foot high or more in some places, but those sheltering beneath awnings found the water creeping up from the brick streets and threatening to overflow where they stood. There was an air downtown of excitement, not unlike what I'd experienced at the beach. Ladies closed parasols to keep them from being pulled away by the wind, and gentlemen stood with hands in their pockets, surveying the skies and nodding at one another like they were old hands at predicting the weather. No one evinced any real concern. The city was built for storms like this. They would come and go and the buildings along The Strand would cling to their granite pilings and resist the incursion, just as they'd resisted the Union Navy and decades of baking summer heat. Having seen the violence of the waves on the other side of the island, I would have urged them to venture inside rather than gawking from the false shelter of covered sidewalks, but the sight of Charlie Fish, splashing up the street in nothing but his long johns did more to put them in motion than any words I could have offered.

We walked several blocks up The Strand, every step a great effort as we tramped through the rising water. Those who noticed us went inside or cleared out of our way in a hurry. Horse-drawn wagons made their way slowly up the street, the horses stomping and anxious. The current pulled against their progress and water climbed their legs. As we neared the docks, I thought of the immigrants we'd seen camped there when we arrived. Had the wind already stolen their tents and scattered their belongings? I hoped they were finding shelter. We passed ship agencies, dry goods stores, a bank with its windows shuttered. The Saturday noon hour had surely passed by now, and I hoped that would drive some of these people home, their business concluded.

Charlie Fish spotted the children before Abigail and me. He howled, lumbered up onto the sidewalk and stalked toward them. Professor Finn yanked Nellie along in his wake with a tight grip on her forearm. She pulled against him, stumbled, and he dragged her forward until she regained her footing. Kentucky Jim held Hank in the crook of his arm, hauling him like a sack of potatoes.

We caught up with our quarry as they headed toward a ramshackle hotel that was popular with sailors and other hard types. Nellie spotted us a second before we were upon them, looked back with dark satisfaction.

Finn and Jim recognized the threat a moment too late.

Finn caught sight of Charlie's massive hand coiled into some approximation of a fist, yelled a warning to his companion. The big man turned his head just in time to catch the blow from Charlie Fish directly in the face.

Kentucky Jim went to the ground, spitting teeth.

Hank hit the sidewalk, rolled off into the deep water running up the street. Climbed back up and grabbed his sister's leg.

"Let her loose!" he said.

Professor Finn found himself caught in a state of pure self-preservation. He released the girl, backed away from Charlie.

Charlie loomed over Jim, determining whether he intended to stay down or needed some more personal attention. I gathered Nellie to me, grabbed Hank's shirt collar and pulled him along too. Finn continued to back away slowly, shaking his head, wondering perhaps if his situation was beyond salvaging. He pressed himself against the front of the hotel, breathing so hard I thought he might pass out. His teeth ground together in a thin white line, the animal inside him coming to the surface.

"Nothing is worth this much trouble," said Finn.

He reached inside his coat, pulled out a pistol, and shot Charlie in the back.

The water hadn't quite crested the sidewalks here, and Charlie went down hard against the concrete. Streaks of dark-blue blood veined out from underneath him as he worked to push himself into a sitting position. Nellie shrieked like she was the one who'd been shot, and I could barely keep her from escaping my arms and lunging at Finn.

Abigail remained calm, raised her rifle in Finn's direction. Hers was a natural motion, a steady hand and a tight fit of the stock against her shoulder. She found her target straight away and pulled the trigger.

The rusty gun failed to fire.

"Well, hell," she said.

Professor Finn still held his pistol and certainly owned the advantage in close combat against Abigail's rifle and my empty fists. But his gun was an antique. Probably something he'd gotten from his grandfather. A single-shot black powder piece that would have been old even back in the war. If he hadn't kept it close beneath his cowhide coat, his powder would never have been dry enough to fire. Abigail understood the situation just as I did. She closed in and hammered her rifle stock against the side of Finn's head before he could cause any more harm.

He screamed and scampered away, hands over his face, so she didn't come at him again. His bowler hat dislodged, sped down the sidewalk like it wanted nothing more to do with him.

"Grab Charlie," said Abigail. "I'll take the kids."

Charlie had managed to sit, but he was dazed and didn't look to be going anywhere under his own power. I hefted him up, put him on my back with his arms around my neck, and dragged him out into the street. Abigail drew the children alongside her, splashing like ducks. Hank was yelling something I couldn't hear now that we'd left the sanctuary of the covered sidewalk and reentered the torrent. Nellie was crying, refused to go anywhere until she saw I had Charlie. We weren't leaving him behind. Finn kept his distance and Jim was just beginning to rise from the damage he'd suffered. We made our exit in haste, before they could regain themselves.

As we navigated through downtown, the water seemed to circle us. We passed a pair of draft horses hitched to a flatbed loaded with lumber. The water surged upward, nearly touched their stomachs. Abigail was forced to lift the children, one in each arm, and for one unsettling moment they bobbed beside her like fishing corks on a lake. Then the water pulled back with such force that the current nearly took me with it.

"Push through it," I said. "Don't stop."

It wasn't far across the island, a mile and a half. Maybe two. But it was hard going. The rain never relented, and the wind was hungry.

As we passed through neighborhoods, we watched slate tiles separate from rooftops, lifted like leaves in an autumn gale. A little girl with brown curls and a blue dress waved from a cupola, high atop one of the grand mansions. The sky turned swiftly from gray to black behind her as storm clouds continued to march in from the Gulf. I had an irrational fear that the wind might tear the cupola from the roof and carry her away, but she remained safely inside, watching us, until we were out of sight.

Charlie Fish was a dead weight on my back and Nellie hadn't stopped crying. She'd lost herself in the chaos and her whisper talk rampaged through my thoughts.

Terror took root.

Charlie's pain settled into my back like I was the one

who'd been shot, and I went down to my knees in the street, Charlie's arms still wrapped around my neck.

Abigail shouted. "Floyd, what's happening?"

Nellie's fear was a bad taste in my mouth, and Abigail's face twisted up like she was tasting it too. Before, the whisper talk had been unsettling but subtle. Now it was a board to the side of my head. *Finn's fingers dug into my forearm as he pulled me down the boardinghouse steps. He yelled in my face, his eyes so close I could see the bloody veins, and the rotten stink of the man caused my stomach to rise up.* Through Nellie, I saw every detail of the kidnapping, and more importantly, I understood what she'd read from her captors' minds. The cold-blooded desperation and hunger. The absolute willingness to kill us all and never miss a single night's sleep. It was a wonder they'd left Abigail alive, and maybe they thought they hadn't. Charlie's wound burned like a tiny sun against my back, and the rain slapped down like hammer blows. I begged Nellie to cut the connection, but she either ignored me or was too lost in the whispering to pay me any mind. Charlie's blood ran hot down my back, and his thoughts chased through the streets and found the ocean. *They were coming. They were so close.* All of this could be made right, and he'd probably heal up, given time, but none of that mattered to him so long as he could look upon his brothers and his sisters and all the others. His yearning was so strong that my eyes started to burn, and I felt like there was no hope I'd ever be happy again.

Most of all, Charlie mourned for his father and mother,

and the thought of absent mothers caused me to choke back a sob. My own mother ran a hand lovingly across my head, and Charlie's mother blossomed out of the darkness with the rumble of the sea beating against the earth. I could almost make out her shape. Hank shook me. He shook Abigail. Maybe he was shaking Nellie, trying to bring her back to the here and now.

"Nellie, please," Hank yelled over the storm. "You're hurting us."

And it all stopped.

Nellie sat beside me in the street, water rising to her chest. "I'm sorry. I got lost."

"Don't be sorry." Abigail stood, lifted Nellie to her feet. I wanted to get moving too, but the memory of pain still stabbed at my back.

Charlie's eyes blinked open. We stared at one another, and I wondered if he'd felt my mother's hand stroking his head.

"We have to go, Floyd," said Abigail. "Storm's bad enough. But for all we know, those men haven't given up."

I finally stood, helped Charlie up. He was bleeding a lot. I took off my shirt, did the best job I could to tie it tight around him and cover the wound.

"You able to come along without me carrying you?"

Charlie seemed to understand. He nodded.

"Let's go then."

I supported him, and together we all limped home.

By the time we reached the boarding house, seawater ran in a deep river down the streets, waist-deep and fighting us every step. There was no longer a question as to the violence of this storm. In the distance, I could see more siding pull away from Murdoch's as the wind gnawed at the world like a dog at a stew bone. Sections of the streetcar trestles had snapped and been torn away, leaving the carcasses to sway and scream beneath the weight of the wind, ready to pull loose and come tumbling inland. The storm growled. Debris clattered against the side of the boarding house, and when we made our way around to the front, we saw that the flowing water had torn away the steps that led up to the door.

I hefted the children up and in through the doorway, one by one. Supported Abigail and Charlie as they climbed inside. Then I fought my way over to Abigail's storage shed at the back of the house, found that the water had already torn off the boards on one side. I felt around and retrieved the long-handled axe that I knew she kept there for just this sort of day.

Back at the front door, I tossed the axe into the house and Abigail helped pull me from the water and over the threshold.

"You can scratch that porch off your to-do list."

We smiled at one another; the relief at being home safe was enough to release some tension, even though worse might be coming.

"You're not going to like what I do to your floor."

"No, I won't," she said. "But you'd better get on with it anyway. Water looks like it's still rising."

Finn and Jim had damaged the door and the top hinge

had partially pulled away. Being left to slap in the wind while we'd been gone hadn't improved matters. We pulled it to, best as we could, but it wasn't likely to stay closed. Rain sounded against the windows, and I regretted not being here earlier to close the outside shutters and board them shut. If that wind got any worse, glass was liable to start flying.

Abigail rolled back the rug, and I set to chopping holes through the pine floor with the axe. Everyone near the beach knew this trick, but hoped they'd never have to use it. The idea was, if you created some holes to let the water flow in, it would rise without lifting the house and carrying it away. Breaking through the floor revealed the water rushing beneath the elevated house, escaping the ocean and racing to fill the island.

I was thankful that the boardinghouse had a second story.

I cut a half dozen holes in the hardwood, spaced out throughout the downstairs. Charlie sat watching from the wingback chair, slumped like he might fall to the floor, and Nellie clung to his leg. Abigail sat in the middle of the floor, soaked and miserable.

We were all nearly broken with exhaustion.

I hadn't realized Hank had run upstairs until he came clomping back down, his big pistol strapped to his hip.

"In case they followed us," he said.

They wouldn't have to follow us. They knew exactly where we were. But they'd have to fight the storm to get here. I wasn't sure they were that determined.

Turns out I was wrong.

We spent half an hour trying to situate the house for the storm as best as we could from the inside. We moved the heavy mahogany cupboard from the kitchen and placed it in front of the large window that faced the ocean. With any luck, it would catch the glass if the wind broke through. We tied the heavy drapes closed across the rest, upstairs and down, and secured the edges to the wall with penny nails. I doubted it would make much difference, but it was better than nothing. The windows shuddered and moaned in their panes.

As Abigail and I were finishing the last bedroom, something roared downstairs. We went down and found that the wind had torn away what was left of the front door, and rain blew sideways through the opening.

"Kids, y'all help Charlie get upstairs," I said.

The temperature was coming down fast and the wind blowing in had already pulled off one of the drapes we'd nailed down and sent it flapping around the parlor like a bat.

"We can't leave them to die," Nellie said.

"Leave who?" I asked. "Hank, help your sister with Charlie."

"I say we shoot them," said Hank.

"Floyd!" Abigail's voice was sharp as a razor.

I turned fast. Saw what everyone else had already seen. Finn and Jim, clinging to the bottom of the door frame with their fingertips. The water was a black, swirling mass, pulling at the two criminals as they fought desperately to hang on to the house. The water had risen to within a foot of the entryway, and in calmer seas they'd have been able to swim up and let themselves in, but the ocean had its arms around them and wouldn't let go. Even Jim, who was the size of an outhouse and strong as a bull, labored in vain against the storm's hold.

"If we don't help them, they'll drown," said Nellie.

"Don't matter none to me," said Hank.

"We have to help them," said Nellie.

"I think she's right," said Abigail.

I shook my head. "Wasn't a few hours ago you were going to shoot him in the head. Now you want to invite them in?"

"There's a difference between defending yourself and letting someone die when you could help them."

"I believe it's a mistake."

"And I believe you're a better person than this, Floyd."

Both of the men hollered for help, barely able to hang on. I knew if I gave it a few seconds, the argument would answer itself. They'd be gone and good riddance.

"If I step on their fingers, they'll just float away," said Hank.

"You'll do no such thing!" said Nellie.

"Well, they'd deserve it."

"Oh hell, then." I knelt down, took Professor Finn's forearm in a two-handed grip, and helped wrestle him into the house. Together, we pulled Jim in next, and the two of them sat on the floor, trying to catch their breath.

Hank unholstered his pistol, waved it at the two men.

"Sit over there on the divan, scoundrels."

"What is it with you people and that descriptor?" asked Finn.

"Put that gun away!" said Abigail.

Hank did as she asked, but the two men crawled across the floor and took a seat on the divan. Finn picked at the lace covering with his grimy fingers. He'd lost his coat and one of his shoes, and the rest of his wet clothes clung to his skinny body tight as tree bark. Jim sulked beside him. His mouth was a red cave where Charlie had hit him, and blood clotted in his woolly beard.

"Thank you kindly for the shelter," said Finn.

"Don't make us regret it," said Abigail.

"I never would." Finn smiled.

"Don't worry, Mr. Betts," said Hank. "I'm a quick draw."

"You better be," I said. "We may require your services."

NELLIE

CHARLIE FISH sat in Mrs. Elder's wingback chair, staining it blue with his blood. He was slumped over to one side, had a grip on the chair so he wouldn't slide off onto the floor. His breathing came in rapid bursts, and his gills made a wet, whistling sound. The bullet had passed clean through him, and Charlie assured me his wound wasn't mortal. It would stitch back together, given time and salt water. But the pain was immense, and no matter how hard he tried to hold it inside, I couldn't help but feel a shadow of that ache in my chest.

We'd become joined tight as two snakes in a basket, and I could feel how weak he was.

Wind raced in through the gaping doorway, chased through the halls like a herd of pigs let loose from a pen. Knocked over candlesticks and rattled the china on the sideboard. Stripped the tablecloth right off the wood. Rain joined the commotion, and the floor grew slick.

We stood around the parlor, watching the two criminals seated on the divan like they were a pair of hungry wolves who'd ambled in through the open door. They were as sodden as the rest of us. One side of Finn's face was lathered in mud. Not a whole lot of Kentucky Jim's face remained, after the way Charlie had hit him. Anger burned like a fever inside them, but Finn kept a wide smile on his face, eager to help us forget their terrible intentions. Eager for us to let down our guard.

None of us would make that mistake again.

"Now that we caught them," said Hank, "what do we do with them?"

"You haven't caught us, child," said Finn.

"You're our prisoners, ain't you?" Hank had his palm on the handle of his pistol, but kept it holstered to comply with Mrs. Elder's wishes.

"That's not how I see it," said Finn.

"Don't engage with these men," I said.

"We can throw you right back in the water," said Hank.

"You might find it harder putting us back out that door than you did helping us in," Finn said.

"If I shoot you enough times," said Hank, "I suspect you won't put up much of a fight."

"Hank! Stop prodding him," I said.

"You should listen to her," said Finn. "Perhaps you're hungry for violence, but you're liable to find that my partner and I are more of a meal than you can manage. The main course, if you will."

"I'm not afraid of you. Not even a little."

"That just shows you're not very smart."

"Enough!" said Mrs. Elder. "Sit there and keep quiet, or we *will* find a way to put you back out that door. You can be sure of that."

"As you wish," said Finn.

Charlie heaved up a mess of blood, bleated a warning. Lucky for the two scoundrels, he was in a bad way. Else I'm sure he'd have killed them where they sat.

"What can we do to help Charlie?" asked Mr. Betts.

"Keep him comfortable," I said. "He'll recover once he's back with his family, in the ocean."

"What if he doesn't make it that long?" said Mr. Betts. "We don't know how soon they'll be here."

"Yes, we do."

Mr. Betts grimaced. He understood what I meant.

The hurricane would not be deterred. I could smell the salt and the blood. Grief clawed at my chest, burrowed down deep into my heart.

Nobody on the island had ever endured the sort of violence that this storm promised. I *understood* the hurricane now. Felt it on a level too deep to articulate, but no less terrible in its reality. The weather we'd endured while crossing the island was nothing but the storm planting seeds for what was to come. The harvest would raze the city to the ground, leaving nothing behind but empty earth and husks of houses, broken loose to traverse the land like tumbleweeds.

Mrs. Elder tried vainly to get the windows covered

again, fighting against the flapping curtains. Her effort might have brought her comfort, but it would amount to very little. Broken windows and wet furniture wouldn't mean anything for much longer.

"May I help you with that?" asked Finn.

"You may sit there in silence and be thankful you're indoors." Mrs. Elder nailed down one of the curtain edges that had come loose and then she began searching the room for the one that had flown away from the side window. Mr. Betts joined in the search.

"Silence is not one of my strong suits, I'm afraid." Finn wiped off some of the muck from his face, tossed it at his feet. "We have common cause now, you know. Virtue or vice means naught to a storm like this one. It will feast on every one of us with the same ravening energy. Aren't we better off forming an alliance, at least until the danger has passed?"

"No, we are not," said Mr. Betts.

"We can assist with the storm preparation," said Finn.

"It won't make any difference," I said.

"Adults are speaking, child," said Finn.

"I only mean to say, we are beyond the point of preparing for the storm. This hurricane is going to swallow you whole, and nothing you can do now is going to change that."

I wasn't entirely certain that was the case, but I enjoyed the flash of fear in Finn's eyes when I said it. Then I thought of the way I'd prodded Mr. O'Casey, and the cost of such childishness, and I wished I'd stayed quiet. Finn struggled to keep his composure, and I felt him peeling away from the divan, ready to lunge. Jim sat beside him, a forgotten boulder. But I knew his stillness came from a place of intense concentration, and no matter his injuries, he could make quick work snapping my neck if I gave him the chance.

Hank read the tension, pulled his pistol.

Finn waved his hands in front of his face, sank back down into the soggy upholstery. "You children are a menace."

"I said I ain't afraid of you," said Hank.

"You *aren't* afraid of him," I said.

"Don't get those men riled up!" said Mr. Betts.

The wind raged with such force through the room that we all resorted to yelling, just to be heard.

Mrs. Elder waved us away from the scoundrels. We'd been creeping closer to them without meaning to. I stepped back, felt warm water run across my ankles. Realized where it was coming from.

"Mr. Betts," I said. "The water's coming in."

The seawater had risen some more. It bubbled up through the holes Mr. Betts had chopped in the floor and spilled through the open threshold like blood from an artery. The water wasn't going to retreat any time soon.

The rush of terror from everyone in the room sent cold needles into my brain.

Professor Finn moaned loud enough that I heard him over the wind. His mind summoned a harrowing image of himself, dead and bloated and floating in the gray deeps.

His limbs were tangled in blue seaweeds that grew up from the pebbled seafloor, and tiny golden fish nibbled at his wide, glassy eyes. Finn squirmed on the divan like an animal caught in a trap, unsure how best to secure his freedom. Desperation cut a trail right through him, and he couldn't shake the sensation of being buried beneath all that ocean water. For a brief second, I felt a stab of pity. Then I remembered how wide his grin had been when Kentucky Jim had struck Mrs. Elder and knocked her to the floor. How hard he'd gripped my arm as he dragged me down the boarding house steps. How he'd shot Charlie in the back. All notions of pity fled my soul like gray doves flushed from the tall grass.

"We must retreat to higher ground," said Finn. "Surely you can't expect us to sit here on this couch until it floats away?"

"How about you stay here, and the rest of us go upstairs," said Hank.

"There's no advantage in being mean," I said.

"Finally, a voice of reason," said Finn.

"Don't think for a moment I'm on your side," I said. "You could sink all the way to the bottom of the ocean, and I won't miss a second of sleep."

"We're all going upstairs." Mr. Betts was afraid, but his fear was a call to action, like he understood the only way to deal with it was to run it over, drive it into the dust. He'd started to get Charlie upstairs before we discovered the scoundrels, clawing at the threshold like drowning varmints, and now he put that plan back into motion. He helped Charlie stand, threw one of Charlie's big arms around his shoulder so he could support his weight. Mrs. Elder helped maneuver them through the rising water, and I could tell she was someplace else in her mind, unwilling to even acknowledge the danger for fear it would take her legs out from under her. She had endured more than most in her life and had no intention of letting it end today.

Kentucky Jim was a different story. He fully expected to die. But he had no intention of leaving the mortal plane without taking the rest of us along. His mind was a riot of blood and smoke and broken bones. He remained stone still, even as the wind blew harder and tossed Mrs. Elder's finery around the room. Only his swollen eyes moved, following Charlie as he staggered across the parlor.

I had advocated for Jim's rescue, but I was far from certain it had been the right thing to do.

Not for the first time, I wondered how he and Finn had managed to get Charlie in that net back at the river. They certainly couldn't have taken him in a fair fight. Might be they tempted him with kindness, pretended to be friendly.

Charlie was kind enough. And he had even less control over his version of whisper talk than I did.

He didn't deserve any of this.

"Hank, please keep your gun trained on these men until Floyd and I can get Charlie upstairs," said Mrs. Elder. "Then we'll come back down to help escort them up too."

Hank beamed like the rising sun, having been granted

permission to keep his gun in his hand. He'd take that thing to the outhouse with him and sleep with it under his pillow if we let him.

I watched them help Charlie up the stairs, wishing for his sake that he'd dive out the window and into the rising flood waters. Swim back out to sea as fast as he could. I had tried to encourage just that, but he'd made it known that even if his people were already here, he did not intend to abandon us. We'd rescued him from these scoundrels, and he wouldn't leave us until the threat subsided.

"Well, I never saw such a thing," said Finn. "Carrying the animals upstairs before helping out good, Christian men."

"He's not an animal," Hank held the pistol at arm's length, gripped with both hands. Sighted down the barrel with one eye closed.

"Hank, he's trying to get a rise out of you. Just ignore him." I pulled Hank back a bit, made sure we were far out of lunging distance.

"Left you children here alone too," said Finn.

"I can swim," I said. "How about you?"

Finn shook his head. "No, can't say that, unfortunately. But I know how to *survive*. I've been in some desperate scrapes. Haven't died yet."

"Good," I said. "I don't wish death on anyone."

He laughed. "I wish all kinds of death on all kinds of people. More often than not, those sorts of wishes come true."

"You do like to hear yourself talk."

"I've admitted as much."

"You might be better off listening for a bit. Hear that rain striking the roof? The sound of that wind howling in through the door? This is only the beginning. The storm's still just whispering. Here soon, it's going to start yelling, and you can scream as loud as you want, nobody is going to hear what you have to say. You can wish for all the death you want, but you can't wish it away. It's coming for you just like all the rest of us."

Wind sped through the room, snapping my skirts like a flag atop a pole. It whistled like a steam engine. Caused the rising water to move quick as a slithering snake across the floorboards. Anger buffeted me. And I realized the whole island was starting to understand the severity of what was happening. I'd just been trying to scare Finn, trying to shut him up, but I understood every word I'd said was true. None of us were liable to survive this storm. All that terror came down on my shoulders like a whole forest of falling pine trees, and desperation muddied my soul.

Whisper talk wasn't going to help now.

I didn't need it to know what Finn and Jim intended. I didn't need it to measure the violence of the hurricane. These were real threats, already inside the house and eager to wreak havoc.

My mother would have figured out a way to save us. She was so much more powerful than I'd ever be.

But she hadn't saved us, had she?

Not all of us, anyway.

The whisper talk overwhelmed me, and I realized that it would continue to drag my mind through the rising swell of fear if I let it. Maybe my mother's blood was a curse, after all. Right then, it threatened to break me down. I'd been born with the power to divine problems, but not one that offered solutions.

The scoundrels were boiling. Just about ready to fight back, to risk Hank's pistol.

Then Mr. Betts was there with his hand on my shoulder, telling me it was time to head upstairs.

I hadn't realized how violently I'd been shaking.

"You look ill, Nellie," said Finn. "If you hadn't disabled my wagon, I'm certain I'd have something that would calm your nerves."

"Get up, you two," said Mr. Betts. "Head on up the stairs and turn right into the first bedroom. Move slow as your old granny headed up the church aisle. You behave like you intend any violence, and the hurricane won't have a chance to kill you."

The scoundrels rose together, crossed slow as spilled molasses toward the staircase.

"What kind of man are you?" asked Finn. "Letting a little boy hold us at gunpoint."

"Kind that knows he's a better shot than me," said Mr. Betts. "I believe you're familiar with his high degree of accuracy?"

Hank still held them at gunpoint. "I promise if I have to shoot you, I'll put the bullet square in the back of your head, so you don't wallow in pain."

Finn gave him a mock bow. "Pleased to be the beneficiary of your kindness."

The scoundrels climbed the stairs without incident, and we followed them up. Already the water in the parlor had risen to my knees, and I began calculating how soon it would reach the upstairs if it continued to rise at the same rate.

Surely it would stop rising at some point.

By the time we reached the upstairs landing, it felt like electricity was moving through my blood. My skin tingled and every inch of me felt heavy, like I was dragging all that oncoming death along behind me. The whisper talk had never felt more of a burden than in that moment, and I wished more than anything that I could cast it aside. Mother could have calmed me down. She could have helped me bundle up all the attacking thoughts and store them away in a safe corner of my mind. But without her, I just wanted the power to vanish. So many people were about to die, and I didn't have the strength to take it all on.

Mr. Betts and Hank ushered the scoundrels into one of the upstairs bedrooms. Mrs. Elder knelt beside me, said something, but the blood hammered in my ears, and I couldn't make out what she was saying.

Despite the rain, I was overcome with images of the boarding house burning. Green flames slithered down the stairway handrail, dripped down the balusters like the fire had become a liquid. At the foot of the stairs, water continued to pour through the doorway, but the water itself burned, green and brilliant and blinding. As long as that front doorway remained open, unguarded, the flames would continue to force their way in, until they burned away every board and beam in the house. Downstairs in the parlor, I could see my mother and father, seated around our old table, every inch of them on fire, skin coming away from their faces and arms like someone was peeling a potato. But they were smiling, holding hands across the table, and Mother's spell pot sat between them. The pot looked to be breathing, inhaling smoke and fire. Trying to suck it all in but unable to keep up with the ferocity of the blaze. Mother and Father appeared untouched by the chaos around them. They burned together happily, looking into each other's eyes like they'd only just met and were falling in love again.

I wanted so much for them to look at me, to see me. But they were beyond all that now.

Tears streaked my face as I watched them burn away. Ashes spun up in the wind, carried through the house like a swarm of gnats. Disappeared into the growing dark.

My parents were gone. The green fire was gone. Only the rising water remained. That and the question of why the whisper talk had shown me all that.

Was I wrong about Mother being able to help?

The world quieted around me. I breathed in the stifling wet air. I smelled the salt, but I also smelled burned tobacco and grain alcohol.

Mrs. Elder was pulling on my arm, coaxing me away

from the upstairs landing, toward the questionable safety of the bedroom. I yanked loose. Took control of myself again.

"Where did you leave your hammer?" I asked.

"What?" The wind sounded like the earth was splitting in half, and Mrs. Elder hollered to be heard.

"Your hammer. I need it."

"You don't need a hammer, Nellie. Come on in the room. We need to shut the door before we blow away."

I reached into the small pocket in my dress, removed the three iron nails, and showed her. "I need the hammer."

Someone else might have ignored my wishes or demanded an explanation, but Mrs. Elder and I understood each other Mr. Betts yelled at us from the bedroom, but Mrs. Elder gave me a long, appraising look before responding.

"Will that help us?" she asked.

"I don't know for sure," I said. "Might be there's something left of my mother's spell."

Mother was always so aware of everything that had gone before, and so much of what would come. Maybe this was part of what she intended for these nails all along.

"Let's go then." Mrs. Elder hurried down the stairs, and I followed. Voices cried out after us, but the wind erased them.

The water in the parlor had risen as high as my knees, and it pulled so hard I had to labor against the undertow to keep from being carried away. I was conscious of where Mr. Betts had cut the holes in the floor, and

I navigated around those spots, so I didn't break a leg. Mrs. Elder waded over to the windowsill in the kitchen where she'd left the hammer. She returned dragging a kitchen chair. I didn't have to tell her what I needed. She read me. *She knew.* She handed me the hammer, positioned the chair near the front door, and held it in place with all her strength.

She didn't need a chair to reach, but it wasn't her responsibility to put the nails in place.

I climbed up on the chair, all three nails clenched in my lips. Hammered them into the top edge of the door frame, one by one.

The doorway looked out toward the ocean, but all I could see was low black clouds and sideways rain. Blackness moved like smoke along the beach, billowed through the streets. Siding pulled away from houses and vanished into the roiling dark. I held the doorframe, braced myself against the wind, and felt all the terror in Galveston flow through me like a river overrunning its banks. But with the nails in place, I could fight back against it. A silver current of hope sliced through the floodwaters, and I swear I saw dozens of wide eyes peering up from the moving sea.

"Is it done?" asked Mrs. Elder.

"Yes, it's done."

Mrs. Elder lifted me off the chair, carried me across the parlor and up the stairs.

We joined the others in the bedroom and waited for our fates to claim us.

FLOYD

We assembled upstairs in the front bedroom where I'd been sleeping. Finn and Jim sat on the edge of the bed like a pair of scolded children while the rest of us stood near the covered front window on the other side of the small room. I thought about stashing the men in a separate bedroom, but the doors had no locks, and I figured we were better off being able to keep an eye on them anyway.

"Don't seem fair they get the bed," said Hank.

"Nobody is going to be sleeping," said Nellie.

"Still don't seem fair."

"I couldn't sleep on this bed anyway," said Finn. "Feels like a slab of granite." He bounced a couple of times and grimaced, to drive home his point.

Blood rose red in Abigail's cheeks. "If the accommodations aren't to your liking, you know the way out the door."

"Or the window," said Hank.

Early night had stolen in with the storm and the

drapes were pulled, so Abigail lit an oil lamp atop the chest of drawers. Ghostly sheets of yellow light clung to the flowered wallpaper, drove shadows into the corners.

"I didn't intend any offense," said Finn.

"Mrs. Elder, I guarantee he meant offense," said Hank.

"Close your mouth, boy." Finn eyed Hank like he was considering whether he was fast enough to take his pistol away before the boy could shoot him.

"Take your own advice," said Abigail.

Kentucky Jim leaned forward, tried to say something with his mangled mouth. We'd have had an easier time understanding Charlie. Jim's jaw was cocked sideways and hung limp as a saddlebag.

"Your friend don't look so good," I said.

Finn smiled. "Yes, well *your* friend looks worse."

He wasn't wrong about that.

Charlie slumped in the corner, gills flaring, black eyes gone big as saucers. Best as I could tell, he'd mostly stopped bleeding, but a low wheeze sounded with every breath he took, and every so often a shudder went through him like an electrical charge. Nellie had said he'd be okay, that his people could help him, but I wasn't entirely sure he'd live long enough to make the family reunion.

"When the storm passes, we'll be escorting you gentlemen to the police station." Abigail took a seat in a chair next to Charlie, put a consoling hand on his back.

"An excellent plan," said Finn. "You attempted to murder me in cold blood, and I'd like to report that. I'm sure there were witnesses."

"We were defending ourselves."

"Not how I see it," said Finn. "I believe my version of the events will be more compelling. You people destroyed my wagon and have tried to shoot me on more than one occasion. Then you turned this unnatural beast loose on me in broad daylight, and what else could I do but shoot the creature to keep it from killing me first? What a misfortune it was to ever cross paths with such a band of brigands."

"I'll tell them the truth," said Nellie.

"They won't believe you," said Finn.

"Yes, they will. I'll show them."

Tension tugged at the room, and I could tell Nellie was using her whisper talk. She conjured up an image of Professor Finn, swaying from a hangman's noose. It seemed suddenly so real, I swear I could smell the stench of his death and hear the rope groaning from the gallows. Finn clutched at his throat, like he could feel it cut into his neck, and he cussed Nellie until she relented.

"Just in case you forgot what happens to men who try to kill children," Nellie said.

"Are you a witch?" asked Finn.

"Are you afraid of witches?" she asked.

"Oh, how I wish for the days when your sort was burned at the stake." Finn tried to tear Nellie down with his stare, but it was all bluster. She had shaken him. He whispered something into Jim's ear, and they both watched Nellie close, like they'd sorted out that she was the more dangerous of the siblings, despite the fact that she was unarmed.

"Quit your whispering," said Hank.

"Now we aren't allowed to speak?" said Finn.

"You aren't allowed to *scheme*," said Hank.

"Don't rile them up any more than they already are." I put a hand on Hank's shoulder, uncertain whether he might do something regrettable.

"I'm not afraid of them," Hank said.

"Nor should you be." Finn found his smile, slipped his innocent face back on like a mask. "You all have a gun, a witch, and a monster. You are fully in command. My friend and I only wish to go on living. That's not so much to ask, is it?"

I didn't give Hank time to answer. "We aren't killers."

"I believe you," said Finn. "But the storm may not show similar restraint."

The wind had grown more violent, so loud now that I realized we were all yelling just to be heard. The boarding house groaned, and you could practically feel the air tightening, squeezing it to death.

I pulled aside the corner of the front window curtain and looked out toward the beach. Murdoch's was gone, either torn completely from existence or hidden away by the black, creeping gloom. Debris spun in the air, slapped at the nearby houses. A bicycle tire struck the side of the boarding house, just beside the window I was looking out of, then careened up and over the roof. Water rushed in from the ocean, like the Gulf of Mexico was a great big soup pot that had been tipped over by a careless giant. It had already climbed midway up the first story of the house and crashed around both sides like river rapids. Dark clouds moved in at such a pace, it was evident the flood would get much worse.

I figured it no longer mattered who had the gun or who had the upper hand. It no longer mattered who had murder or fear or kindness in their heart. The storm presided over us all, and the storm alone would decide who lived and who died.

"How does it look?" asked Abigail.

"Not good," I said. "Water's getting deeper and deeper. I've never seen a storm like this one."

The temperature was dropping fast, but we were all sweating, caught up together like condemned prisoners in one crowded cell. The walls around us shuddered, and the last few slivers of daylight that had been edging in around the curtains faded away.

"Black night falls," said Finn. "Be surprised if any of us lives through to morning."

"We'll be fine," I said.

I'd come to realize that probably wasn't true, but there was no benefit in frightening everyone more than they already were.

Finn sat on the bed, anxious and fidgeting with a stray thread on the patchwork quilt. Jim sat close beside him, brooding and sullen, staring straight at Hank like he was still figuring how he could get the gun. Blood trailed down his broken chin, and the oil lamp colored his face a sickly, monstrous yellow. The children huddled close to Charlie. He'd started up with that keening sound again, but I could barely hear it over the raging wind. Nellie pressed her face against his chest, listening for his heartbeat, and Hank clung to his sister like he was afraid the storm would carry her away without him. I knelt beside Abigail's chair and held her hand. I put my mouth up close to her ear and spoke so nobody else could hear.

"I don't believe these men will be content with the storm killing us," I said. "The big one won't be satisfied until he has some payback."

"Well, if they plan to kill us before the storm does, they better get to it quick," she said.

I laughed, but the sound was so out of place that it dissipated like smoke before I could take any joy from it.

"This is a bad time to tell you I love you," I said.

"It sure is. You'd best save that talk for later."

"But it's a conversation you'd be willing to have?"

"I think you know I would."

"I very much hope I survive then, Mrs. Elder."

It was Abigail's turn to laugh, but hers left in a hurry too. "Listen, if you and I are all we appear to be, then I need to be honest with you about something. I killed my husband. He tried to harm me, and I harmed him first. Understand there was a meanness to him, and it wasn't the first time he put his hands on me. A person can only take so much. I'm telling you this to confess my soul in case we die, though I'm not sorry I did it. But I'm mostly telling you so you'll know I can do what needs to be done here if the need arises. And I'm afraid it might."

"I don't know what to say, Abigail. I'm sorry."

Tears welled in her eyes, caught the flickering lamplight. "Nothing to be sorry about. That's not why I'm telling you all this. I'm just saying, if those men try to harm the children again, I will not have a problem killing either one of them. I know they aren't mine, but I've grown fond of them both, enough that I can look to the other side of this mess and see us all having a life together. Some ugly part of me wishes they'd never come here. A few days ago, I'd never even met them, and now just the thought of something bad happening to them scares me silly. I'm not sure I'd be able to endure that sort of pain."

"Nothing's going to happen to them," I said.

"I don't need you to lie to me," she said. "We both know that neither one of us can promise that."

"I guess not. But I feel like we're going to get our chance at that life."

"This storm doesn't care about feelings."

"No, but I got to hang on to *something*."

"I love you, Floyd."

"You know we don't have time for that."

This time Abigail's laughter was genuine. It filled her eyes and reddened her face. I wanted nothing more in that moment than to spend the rest of my life listening to her laugh.

We all sat there for what might have been an hour, each of us contemplating our fates and watching the terror in one another's eyes as the storm grew stronger. The house developed a constant shudder as the storm worked at its roots like a weed, trying to pull it loose from the soil. Debris battered the walls, and I knew it wouldn't be long before the windows shattered and the storm came inside. Rivulets of water crawled across the floorboards, and I realized that the downstairs was completely underwater. The ocean had reached the top of the stairs. It flowed under the bedroom door and bubbled up through the floor. The house shook harder and suddenly lurched to one side.

Right then, Charlie started screaming.

He brushed the children off him, stood and lumbered over to the window facing the street. Charlie tore off the window covering and put a hand on the glass to steady himself. The sudden motion caused the two scoundrels to stand, but Hank already had his gun drawn and pointed in their direction. The floor rumbled beneath his boots, and I hoped to hell he didn't drop the gun. Charlie struggled to breathe normally, and his screaming came in sharp blasts of expelled air, like a wheezy old man. Everyone seemed to be hollering at once, but all I could hear was that whistle coming from Charlie. I hustled over beside him so I could see what had drawn him to the window.

Outside, it was so much worse than I'd imagined.

The neighborhood was at sea. Black ocean water surged inland, carrying a knot of palm trees and bent train trestles past the window as we watched. Snapped timbers rode the wind, and bricks swarmed in the air like hornets. Lamplight burned from a few second-story windows, and I could make out people gathered at a few of them, looking back at us. Just as terrified and just as doomed. Charlie kept screaming, like he was calling out to them across the stormy divide. Any thought that we might escape to the rooftops if the water rose higher was banished. Iron fence posts stabbed into the roof across the street like it was a pincushion, and the wind lifted another roof completely into the air as we watched. It rose into the heavens, hauling half a wall behind it. The wind sounded like a sawmill as it cut across the island. In the distance, we saw the top story of a house floating away, like a ship lost on stormy seas.

There was nothing like this hurricane in our memories. This was a biblical cleansing of everything living on our island.

I was breathing so hard, I grew light-headed. I held on to Charlie like he might anchor me to the spot, but he was unsteady on his feet too. Still, when the house shuddered again, he grabbed my arm and kept me from toppling over. He turned me back to the window, motioned for me to look again, and I saw what had drawn him there.

Heads, bobbing in the water. Fish faces, just like Charlie's, at least a dozen. His family, come to take him home. They swam against the angry flow, round, black eyes watching us, waiting for Charlie to join them.

He could have opened the window, gone with his family, but he stood there, leaking blue blood and gasping for breath, unwilling to leave us at the mercy of these killers.

I won't ever forget that.

Something snapped and the house tilted some more. We were leaning a good twenty degrees to one side now, and all of us grabbed on to something solid, for all the good it would do if the storm decided to carry the house away. Kentucky Jim screamed through his busted jaw and Hank tried to keep the pistol trained on him. Finn slipped his mask again, and nothing remained but an animal, bent on survival at any cost. They stalked toward Abigail and the kids, gun be damned, and when Hank pulled the trigger, the bullet sang past Jim's hip and pinged off the brass bedpost. Finn lunged, grabbed Hank by the hair and drove him to the ground. All of this as the house wrenched in the opposite direction, sending everyone tumbling across the floor. The oil lamp plunged into the rising water, and we were in near darkness.

Blood thrummed in my ears as the storm tightened around the house.

I was trying to get back to my feet, searching for the two scoundrels, when the front window shattered. Glass and shredded curtains crashed through the room, and seconds later, the other window broke open, creating a crosswind that nearly pulled me out into the storm. Hank wrestled loose from Finn, turned, and put a bullet in his gut. Finn might have screamed, but I couldn't hear him. He rolled away, grabbed at Nellie's ankles like she might help him. Abigail stomped down on his wrist and pulled Nellie out of reach.

Kentucky Jim shoved Abigail aside, lifted Hank up

from the floor, and yanked the gun from his hand. It fell and disappeared beneath the water.

The house pitched and turned, and I had to hold on to the windowpane to keep from falling again. The chest of drawers toppled and fell, and the bed skidded across the room, pinning Professor Finn to the wall.

Charlie was still on the ground, but he crawled toward Kentucky Jim, knocking aside the bedside table as it slid into his path. Nellie and Abigail climbed onto the bed and held on.

Kentucky Jim stepped through the chaos, like the storm was no more than a summer breeze, then he heaved Hank out the open window and into the sea.

Nellie's scream cut through us all like gunfire.

I lost my grip on the windowsill and splashed down into the water. It had risen halfway up the legs of the brass bed and I might have drowned there on the floor if Abigail hadn't reached down and pulled me up onto the mattress with her. She had a bedsheet wound up like a rope and she shoved Nellie into my arms and started lashing her to me with the sheet. Nellie was still screaming, and I could feel her misery digging into my brain. When Abigail finished, Nellie's head was on my shoulder, and she was bound tight against my chest.

"Don't let her go," yelled Abigail. "Don't lose her!"

Abigail gripped the bedrail, knowing the house was about to tear loose and float away. Professor Finn had figured this out too, and he wrapped his arms around the headboard.

"I'll tie you to us too!" I snatched up the quilt and started trying to wrap it around Abigail somehow, but it wasn't long enough. One of the curtains had caught up on the bed's legs, and I reached down for it. Kentucky Jim moved in like a shark, yanked me from the bed and threw me to the ground. Nellie and I splashed into the water, and Jim stomped down on my left arm so hard I could hear the snap over the sound of the wind. He put his boot on my face, pressed my head down under the water and held me there. Nellie went under with me.

We'd have both been dead if not for Charlie.

After a few seconds, the pressure relented and I sat up, gasping for air. Charlie was still on the ground, but he was pummeling the back of Jim's head, driving his face into the water and against the floorboards. Charlie gasped and wheezed, but he wouldn't relent until Kentucky Jim went still.

Abigail reached down, pulled me up onto the bed again. My broken arm hung loose, but I couldn't feel any pain. I knew that would come, but right now I could only focus on keeping us all alive.

I reached for the curtain again but couldn't get it unwound from the bed. Nellie cried and thrashed against me, reaching out toward Charlie. Her whisper talk pinned us all in place, her voice screaming in our minds *help him help him help him help him help him* and we understood she meant her brother, but the house pitched again, and it was all we could do to hang on to the bed and not be swept away as water rushed in through the windows.

Abigail grabbed the bed as the water lifted it up, and I held on to her with my one good arm. Something boomed from underneath the water. The house spun like a top and lurched up, suddenly cut loose from the foundation and at the mercy of the current. Nellie kept insisting *help him help him help him help him help him* and I saw Charlie bobbing in the water, torn between helping Nellie and following her wishes. Finally, he swam out what was left of the front window and dove below the water just as the roof peeled away and the walls of the boardinghouse collapsed around us.

The walls quickly broke into pieces and sped off in the flow. The bed got caught up with the debris and we rode with it.

The storm swept everything along—houses, trees, wagons, horses, broken bodies—all carried by the torrent. I couldn't concentrate on anything but keeping my one-handed grip on the mattress. Splintered wood, masonry, and all manner of twisted metal shredded the air, tearing through treetops and shearing the tops off houses that hadn't yet collapsed. Splinters sliced open my skin and I kept my head down, knowing it would be blind luck if I made it through this without the wind driving a six-foot length of lumber through my chest. The mattress pitched and fell as the wind tried to lift us away, and if we hadn't been wedged up beneath a section of clapboard siding, we'd have taken flight.

I have no idea how long we rode the water, but after a time I realized we'd stopped moving and I opened my eyes. Our mattress and a few bent pieces of the brass bed had come to rest in the clutches of a massive tree branch. A mound of debris at least thirty feet across had become lodged in a space between the tree and one of the two-story brick mansions in the middle of the island. Only the roof was still visible, but it was sturdy enough that it held through the storm. Water broke against our pile of flotsam, but we didn't move. Rain came at us sideways, but the mansion shielded us from the worst of the wind. At the very least, it kept us from being carried away.

Nellie was still tied to my chest. Her eyes were closed, though I couldn't tell if she was passed out, terrified, or something worse.

My arm was in pain now and I could feel the broken bones shifting underneath the skin. I sat up on the mattress and saw Finn clinging to the mound of debris a few feet away. He had hold of a fencepost, bound up in a chain, his legs kicking in the water. His mouth was open, screaming, and a few of his words carried through the din. *Storm. Hell. Too much blood. Going to kill that girl.* I don't know where he got it, but he had a knife in his hand, and he started to pull himself from the water, slashing out at us even though he wasn't nearly close enough to reach. Blood poured from his mouth, but he grinned, confident that he had us and there was nowhere we could go. He crawled up the mountain of debris, ignored the bruising rain and the pain he must have felt from the bullet wound in his belly. He kept on smiling. *Not going to Hell by myself. No, sir. All the little witch's fault. My fish man, not yours*. I didn't have the strength to fight him away. I'd do my best, but there was nowhere to go. He was as good as dead too, but it wouldn't take much for him to put that knife in both of us.

Nellie would die. I would die.

Finn moved slow, but he progressed. Grinning and bloody and cursing us every inch. I kicked out at him, but he stabbed at my foot. Got close to us, close enough to cut. Close enough to kill.

He laughed, stuck that knife deep in my calf.

Three fish people broke from the water and scampered up the debris pile. Not Charlie, but his kin. Wet shadows in the darkness. Finn wiggled the knife loose, raised it up again, but the creatures drug him down the slope and into the water before he could do any more damage.

Nellie tried to pull away from me, and I realized she was awake. The fish people watched her with wide, black eyes, and she returned the stare. They bleated and howled and hissed, stationary in the flow, as if the surging storm had no claim over them. One of them had an arm around Finn's neck, keeping the struggling man from escaping, and they listened intently as Nellie pressed her mind together with theirs. I don't know what she told them. But they communicated this way for a long time, and Nellie kept glancing out toward the open ocean. In the end, Nellie was crying and nodding, and she turned away from the fish people, buried her face in my chest so she didn't have to watch when they pulled Professor Finn underneath the water, and kept him there for good.

I still don't know what Nellie said to them, and I never asked.

She cried for a while, and I let her, holding us both to the mattress as best as I could while the wind kept chewing away the world around us.

We remained that way a very long time before she spoke, and when she did, I realized how focused I'd been on keeping Nellie alive, at the expense of all else.

"Mr. Betts," she said. "Where's Mrs. Elder?"

"Oh, Lord."

I started crying, and Nellie with me. I didn't care if I died there on that mountain of broken things. Better than spending the rest of my life digging through it to find everything I'd lost.

Sunday morning brought sunshine and relentless heat, just another summer day in Galveston if not for the complete ruin that daylight revealed.

I untied Nellie and helped her climb down from the nest of broken boards where we'd spent the night, baking in the returning heat and sickened by the stench of sea rot and death. The redbrick mansion that had stopped our progress was still standing, but most of the city had been flattened from the ocean to downtown. Broken lumber scattered like kindling, thrust up in places as if someone was planning a giant bonfire. Mountains of shredded wood that used to be houses marked where the streets used to run. Water fled back toward the bay and the ocean, loud in its retreat as it coursed beneath layers of silt and twisted trees and crushed cinder blocks. There was no ground where we were, just destruction to step through cautiously, so I hefted Nellie with my one good arm and carried her across Galveston's scattered bones. Every step revealed another horror, another broken body, and I asked Nellie to keep her eyes closed tight until I could carry her away from this.

But where was there to go?

Rats scavenged in the aftermath, and I wondered how they'd managed to survive and thrive. We encountered people too, all looking for their families. Searching for things they'd never find again.

How many dead? Thousands to be sure.

I didn't know where to go. Men's voices shouted from the direction of The Strand, and I could hear someone crying not too far in the distance. No doubt some authority would be taking charge, keeping track of all the dead with a pencil and ledger and posting those names on the wall of the police station, if it was still standing. But there were things I was afraid to learn, and the wall of debris stood so high between us and The Strand, that I had an excuse to avoid the truth for a bit longer. I started back toward the beach, picking my way through the dangerous rubble. No destination remained for us, but Nellie fell asleep again, and I could hear waves against the sand and seagull screams, and I wanted to be away from this place. My home was gone, *our* home was gone, but the beach drew me to it for lack of anywhere better to go.

A few people were shifting things around, searching for survivors. I should have done the same, but the little girl I carried required protection, and I had people I hoped to find myself. I struggled through wood and rope and coils of electrical cable, shoved aside a door painted a happy shade of green that had, no doubt, hung proudly from its owner's front door, not ten hours ago. I stumbled over a section of picket fencing and nearly dropped Nellie into a nest of nails and corrugated iron. We crossed a landscape filled with dead dogs and other unrecognizable, bloody things, and more torn faces staring sightlessly at the blue sky than I care to remember. After a time—two hours, three, hard to say—we came to where I remember the boardinghouse had stood.

Best I could tell anyway.

Nothing remained of any of the houses this close to the beach, not even the brick columns that we'd foolishly thought would elevate us above the flood.

A few palm trees stood nearby, stripped of their foliage, and bent to one side. Kentucky Jim was bound to one of them with some netting blown in from the Gulf. His broken jaw had been torn away completely and his head turned too far to the left, like the storm had tried to twist it off. I don't know if Charlie killed him in the bedroom, or if the storm finished the job, but either way, he was just as dead. His head was turned so that it faced the ocean, one arm at his side, the other jutting out at a backward angle with red bone punching through his shoulder. He hung there with his dead eyes open, a scarecrow to frighten away the next storm that threatened the island.

Nellie was awake now, so I put her down, turned her away from the dead man. But there really wasn't any direction she could look without seeing someone in just as bad a shape.

"Can we go to the beach?" she asked.

"We sure can," I said.

We walked the last little stretch to the beach and saw the water was already hauling away some of the debris. I found a place that was mostly clear, and we sat down in the mud and seaweed. Nellie's hair was plastered to her face with grime, and I couldn't count all the cut, bloodied places on her arms and legs and cheeks. I drew her in close to me, and we looked out over the water. Sunlight rained down, so eager and so bright that the whiteness gleaming off the waves was enough to blind you.

"Everything will be okay," said Nellie.

I wanted to believe her. I wanted to believe that Charlie and his friends had pulled Hank and Abigail from the deeps and held them afloat until the storm died off. I wanted to believe that if we waited here long enough, they'd come strolling up the beach, laughing. They'd join us in the sand, and we could make plans for the future. I closed my eyes against the wind, against reality, and did my best to imagine it.

We'd build another house and paint it bright blue.

We'd build a life together, all four of us.

Maybe Nellie saw all of this, or maybe she was lying to herself to keep from facing the truth.

"Nellie, I don't think you can know that."

"Open your eyes, Mr. Betts."

I did, and saw Abigail standing not ten feet away, ankle deep in the mud. Sodden and bloody, but alive. She had a hand up to shield her eyes from the sun, and she looked out over the ocean, like she was making sure the storm had really gone. I called her name, and when she spotted us, her face lit up with a look of relief and happiness, and what I hoped was love.

"Nellie, you may be right about things," I said.

Nellie looked up and down the beach. Searching.

"I guess we'll have to wait and see."

EPILOGUE: 1932

ON THE MORNING I left Galveston, hurricane winds knocked out the electricity. I was sipping hot coffee at the kitchen table, waiting for my toaster to pop, when the brass fixture hanging overhead flickered, and then went dark. Somewhere the sun was rising, but the gray morning promised to keep it hidden. Wind rattled the house. The picture window facing the beach was smeared with seawater. Far out in the Gulf, the ocean pitched like a rodeo bull. And when the waves forced their way up the beach, they met the concrete seawall in a violent collision. Water launched skyward like a massive sea creature breaching the surface.

The seawall held the ocean at bay.

Mr. Betts had built this tall blue house for us even closer to the shore than the old one had stood. Placed it there in quiet defiance of fate.

We had endured other hurricanes, but nothing would ever match the Great Storm of 1900.

I pushed my chair back from the table, decided I wasn't hungry anyway. Best to get moving, just in case. There was no point in pinning my hair, so I left it in untidy weaves that flowed down my cheeks and neck. I didn't bother with shoes either. I wore my favorite blue sundress with polka dots, and a bluebonnet brooch Mrs. Elder had gifted me years ago, pinned through a buttonhole. I was only a few years older than she'd been when I first came to Galveston, but I felt so much more tired than she'd seemed at the time. I felt rubbed raw by the sea. Broken by the heavy air and the punishing sun. And my whisper talk kept the past so terribly close.

Galveston was often a paradise, but memories of the dead dwelled in every murky alleyway, in the tree-lined gardens along the esplanades; on the long beaches and wedged in the eaves of every surviving brick mansion.

Galveston had never recovered from the Great Storm.

Her people were likewise damaged.

A brutal burst of wind met me when I opened the front door, but I pressed forward and down the steps into the yard. I didn't bother locking the door behind me. I lived alone, Mr. Betts having passed away some years back, and Mrs. Elder preceding him in death by a scant six months. They never married, but I believe they always loved each other. They managed the new boardinghouse together, and remained boon companions, but the hurricane that had stripped so much life from the island had taken a measure of our souls away with it too. Regret tied us in knots, and the dead haunted the streets, left us feeling guilty to still be alive.

I headed toward the beach, enjoying the warm mist on my head and shoulders. Wind crashed down, but it wasn't strong enough to deter me. The heart of the hurricane hadn't arrived yet. I saw a few people hammering boards across windows and otherwise preparing for the storm, but most everyone had fled inside already, even those who had no memory of the Great Storm. That day lived in the island's blood. Children grew up hearing horror stories, as if the hurricane was some sort of boogeyman who would one day come back, catch them in its claws, and carry them out to sea.

I wasn't entirely sure that was just a story.

A red Ford truck sped down the boulevard running parallel to the shore, whitewall tires throwing up water. A Packard full of well-dressed tourists came from the other direction, all of them laughing and pointing toward the violent swells. I waited for them to pass, then crossed the street toward the beach.

The concrete seawall had been built in the immediate aftermath of the Great Storm. It stood seventeen feet tall along this stretch of beach and ran for miles in both directions. To accommodate the height of the wall, the elevation of the island had been raised. Even structures that had survived the storm were lifted and repositioned, landing them anywhere from eight to seventeen feet higher than they had stood previously. The base of the wall was sixteen feet thick, and the beachward face curved upward so it might scoop the attacking waters into the sky and usher them back out to sea. The top of the wall was a wide sidewalk, a popular destination for beach strolls and bicycle rides, and when I crossed the boulevard, I stood there on that perch that overlooked the rolling beaches and the vastness of the Gulf.

Swells continued to spray upward, and I stayed just beyond their reach. The wall snaked up the beach, and I could see similar sprays of water all along the length of it. I'd grown confident in this marvel of engineering over the years, but there was a part of me that remained wary of the ocean's power. The part that had seen upward of ten thousand people perish in a single day, and the part that had endured the horrifying weeks that followed.

There is no elegant way to dispose of so many bodies. It was thought they could be buried at sea, so men loaded a host of corpses onto flattop boats, sailed out to deep waters, and pushed them overboard. But when those same bodies came washing up on the beaches, there was no solution but to organize press gang crews to dig trenches for mass graves, and to burn down piles of debris rather than search beneath them for souls who were surely dead. There was a dearth of food and clean water, no medicine, and no contact with the outside world for days. The train trestle to the mainland washed away, and the telegram lines were gone, so there was no way to summon assistance. When it was finally discovered what happened to Galveston, relief came from all corners, but people who landed on the island were met with the putrid smell of decaying bodies, and the haunted eyes of a homeless, broken population.

Sargent Shelby and his officers punished corpse robbers, shooting many of them on sight, and they oversaw a running list of the living and the dead. They posted it on the front of the police station, which had escaped with only damage to the roof, and every day people would crowd around to read the names and pray for good news. Mr. Betts and I made pilgrimages there every day too. We dug through wreckage, questioned everyone we met, trudged from one end of the island to the other.

But we never found out what happened to Hank.

In the intervening years, I built a life for him in my mind. He fought in France, served in the bloody trenches, and returned home with a chest full of gleaming medals thanks to his astonishing marksmanship. He married a pretty girl with a quick wit and a witchy personality, and she gave him a rowdy little boy with muddy brown hair and no end of sass. He won and lost several fortunes, wildcatting in the East Texas oil fields. Every time I closed my eyes, I could smell the grease and sweat, and hear his laughter. I could see Father's old pistol holstered low against Hank's hip, no longer an oversize plaything, but a memory of the dead that he kept close to himself. And I could see the coral-colored bungalow that he built for his family when they came home to Galveston. He lived there, content with the rise and fall of the ocean echoing through the hallways, until old age finally claimed him and carried him away into the mystery.

How I wished all that had happened.

But magic wasn't a cure-all. I'd figured out that much over the years. Mother's spell saved Hank and me from the fury of Old Cypress, plucked us from the fire. But any residual magic the nails might have contained left the world when she did. They served as a sort of talisman, I guess, something to give me hope and keep me moving forward in the wake of the tragedy. But more than anything, they'd been a distraction. A source of false hope. The memory of myself as a little girl, splashing through the flood waters, hurrying to hammer in the nails over the doorway, dredged up more disappointment than I could contain. I was so convinced Mother had a greater plan, that she knew what was coming for us and had provided a path to safety once again. I often wondered, if I'd devoted my energy to the more practical matters of keeping Hank safe, would he have lived that life I wanted for him? When I was truthful with myself, I believed nothing could have been done. For Hank. For any of them. But that truth didn't keep the guilt at bay.

All those dead people haunted my days, Hank more often than most. He argued with me in my sleep, peered out from windows every time I walked up to the grocery. I could hear his laughter echo in the streets. The love he held for me still warmed my insides, and his mischievous grin was seared in my memory like a photograph. He never left the island. None of them did. All those drowned souls were bound to this place. They cried in the deep night and begged me for help.

I could do nothing for them, but I always listened.

The wind tore at my dress and yanked my hair. I struggled against it to keep from being blown back inland. The concrete was hot beneath my bare feet, and the sea spray kissed my face. I stood at the top of a wide stairway that led from the seawall sidewalk down to the beach. Waves hammered against it, pulled back, then returned to swallow the stairs again.

I listened to the ocean cry.

I listened for Charlie.

He was the one who rescued Mrs. Elder from the storm, swam her to shelter. She told me Charlie helped her climb through the third-story window of the bank building on The Strand, then dove back under the water, presumably to look for Hank. It was the last any of us had seen of him.

Charlie going home had been the plan since the day we met, but I hadn't reckoned on the toll that losing him would take. We had become tangled together so tightly, there was no undoing the knot. He was gone, but his absence nagged at me like a sore tooth. His whisper talk called to mine, lured me to the ocean with deep-blue promises. No matter if life was good or life was hard, I found myself longing to follow wherever he'd gone. Even when Mrs. Elder and Mr. Betts were alive, and I still enjoyed the comfort of my rebuilt family, there were days when I wanted nothing more than to walk into the ocean and never come back. Charlie hadn't done anything intentional, but he'd set a hook in me with his magic during our time together, and it was impossible to resist.

Every time the wind picked up, I'd lie in bed and listen to the ocean. I'd fall asleep and dream of heaven. Paradise was a whirlpool of unnatural green and gold coral reefs, phosphorescent flowers and palaces cut into the heart of undersea caverns. Flurries of fish moved like leaves on the breeze. Charlie and his family were there. My parents were there, waiting to see me again. Then I'd awaken, and heaven would be gone. Sunlight would bleed through the windows and sea birds would call from the beach. When Mrs. Elder and Mr. Betts were still alive, I'd smell breakfast downstairs and hear the two people I loved most in the world laughing and puttering about and enjoying one another. And it was wonderful. But it didn't change the hollowness Charlie had left inside me. Only a reunion with Charlie would ever fill those dark places with golden life. And so, every time storms blew in and the sea came alive, I'd walk down to the shoreline and wait for him.

This time, he was close. I could feel him.

I stood atop the seawall, body trembling. I inhaled the salty air, reached out with my whisper talk, let my mind dive deep beneath the water. Calling. Searching. Begging for understanding. I screamed into the wind. And someone screamed back. The ocean advanced slowly, like night falling across the world. A wall of water rose from the Gulf, higher than the seawall, higher than heaven. And when I stared into the beautiful blue face of it, I found the answer to every question I'd ever asked.

I closed my eyes. Smiled.

And held out my hand so Charlie could take me home.

AFTERWORD

None of the characters in this book are real.

But the storm is.

The city of Galveston is situated on a barrier island, just off the coast of Texas. In the late nineteenth century, it was the state's primary port, and one of the most modern cities in the country. On September 8, 1900, a hurricane changed all that. A hurricane so severe, it came ashore with sustained winds of 145 miles per hour and a rapidly moving fifteen-foot storm surge. A morning that began with cloudy skies and most of the population unconcerned about the approaching storm ended in mass death and close to seven thousand buildings destroyed. More than a quarter of Galveston's residents were left homeless, and the trajectory of the city had been changed forever. Death tolls vary, but it's believed between six thousand and ten thousand people died. The Great Storm is still the deadliest natural disaster in United States history.

On that Saturday in September, Galveston existed at a tipping point in time. Modern cities with electric lights lived right alongside medicine wagons and wild west shows. Automobiles were on the horizon, and airplanes would soon follow, but horse-drawn wagons still dominated the day, and in Texas, the Old West had not yet given way to a future of ubiquitous oil wells and gleaming skyscrapers. Yet every eye in Galveston was already looking to that future. Many believed that no storm could seriously threaten such a grand city. And while it was understood that a strong storm approached from the Gulf, storms had come and gone before, and many meteorologists believed it would turn toward Florida. Morning brought heavy waves crashing against the beach, but the sun could still be seen between the low, creeping clouds. By the time rain started to fall and the streets began to flood, it was too late to do anything but to seek shelter and hold on. When the storm surge came, it carried across the island, all the way to the bay, and Galveston's dreams of the future were buried in the ocean.

Many brick and iron buildings survived, but wooden houses were reduced to splinters, plucked from their foundations and carried away. Two dozen churches, several schools, and the Catholic orphanage were all destroyed. The storm carried off telegraph poles, electrical lines, and the elevated railroad tracks connecting Galveston to the mainland. When Sunday dawned, the city was largely rubble, strewn with bodies, and with no way for people to seek help. There was no food, there was no clean water. The disaster spread miles inland along the Texas coast, and though state officials understood what must have happened in Galveston, several days passed before outside help could arrive. The dead were too numerous to bury. Attempts were made to ferry them out into the Gulf for a burial at sea, but when bodies began returning in the surf, they were eventually burned in pyres along the beach. Galveston was in ruins, and what the survivors endured was a horror.

People lived in tents, or built quick shelters from salvaged lumber, and the city was eventually rebuilt. To prevent another disaster, Galveston constructed a tall concrete seawall along the beach, which necessitated raising much of the city to a higher elevation. While Galveston struggled to restore itself, Houston seized the advantage, became the center of commerce for Southeast Texas, and, by dredging a deep ship channel, became the state's primary port as well. The discovery of oil near Beaumont, just a few months after the hurricane, propelled Texas forward into that dreamed future, and Houston led the way.

But Galveston remains.

Today, the city is a popular tourist spot, adjacent to the sprawling Houston metro area. The seawall is home to bicycles and strollers, beach shops and seafood restaurants. Seagulls call and children splash in the surf. Tourists can stroll through The Strand, where the stoutest buildings still stand, and if they arrive in December, they may be treated to Dickens on The Strand, a celebration of the Victorian lifestyle that dominated before the hurricane. Cruise ships dock nearby, and children are drawn to

Moody Gardens, where they can visit three towering pyramids full of rainforest animals, sea life, and science experiments. Historic sailing ships and World War II airplanes sit in close quarters with fishing piers and giant waterslides. Late night ghost tours meander along haunted boulevards. Antique stores and hidden night-spots appear around every corner, and the Galveston Bookshop has a great selection of local history, and a fantastic assortment of old science fiction and fantasy novels. All those beautiful, brightly painted houses were rebuilt long ago, and though few of them predate the storm, they have aged into fine old residents of the island.

With all these attractions, Galveston visitors can be forgiven for not knowing about the island's painful history. But even though the Great Storm happened more than 120 years ago, it's still close at hand, if you go looking for it. Buildings that predate the year 1900 bear placards marking them as hurricane survivors, and tour guides will remark on which of the old mansions were lifted seventeen feet above their original elevation. A statue of remembrance stands along the beach, commemorating the dead, and the sound of the hungry ocean is never far away. But for the most part, Galveston looks to the future. The storm stole the old city, but it left the heart of the place behind.

The island continues to be stalked by hurricanes, but none have ever approached the casualties left behind by the Great Storm. That is not to say subsequent storms haven't been severe. The Freeport Hurricane of 1932 that occurs in the epilogue of this book made landfall just down the coast from Galveston. It arrived with up to 150-mile-per-hour winds, bringing wind damage and power outages to Galveston, and flooding the causeway that connected the island to the mainland. In 2008, Hurricane Ike followed a path similar to the 1900 hurricane, crashed into the Texas coast with a massive storm surge, and set floodwaters loose through the streets of Galveston. Businesses along The Strand have markers on the wall showing just how high the water flowed in off the bay. In 2017, Hurricane Harvey made landfall down the coast from Galveston, bringing widespread flooding along the coast and into Louisiana, including more than forty inches of rain in some locations, necessitating rescue operations in Beaumont, Houston, and elsewhere.

Hurricanes and tropical storms threaten from the Gulf of Mexico every year, and dozens have impacted Galveston and the Texas coast in the decades since the Great Storm made landfall. On average, Galveston has a close call with a powerful hurricane every three years and suffers a direct strike every nine years. And residents can expect a hurricane with the intensity of the Great Storm, about every thirty years. Predicting these storms is much easier now; we can often pinpoint landfall before the eye reaches shore. We can raise buildings tough enough to withstand hurricane winds, and nail plywood over our windows. We can load our loved ones and our pets into cars and join thousands of others in mass evacuations. But there is no way to turn the storms away, to send them raging back out to sea, and so cities like Galveston will forever be at their mercy, no matter how accurate our predictions, no matter how tall we build our seawalls.

Tropical storms have always been a way of life along the coast. They visited the Karankawa who first called Galveston Island home, and they harried Jean Lafitte, the pirate who claimed the island as a base for his smuggling operation. The flags of Mexico and the Republic of Texas have snapped in the approach of violent tropical winds. And every summer, when hurricane season comes to call, the people of Galveston carry on with their lives. They aren't afraid, and they don't dwell on long ago hurricanes, but they do keep one eye on the weather.

No one expects another hurricane like the Great Storm.

But whatever happens, Galveston will endure.

ACKNOWLEDGMENTS

The Legend of Charlie Fish started out life in a much different form, and grew into the book it became due to the hard work and support of some fantastic folks. Thanks to Rick Klaw for seeing more in this story and helping me find what was missing. Thanks to Jodi Henry, Derek Austin Johnson, and Jaime Lee Moyer for reading this in beta form and providing valuable insights. Thanks to my agent, Kris O'Higgins, for the guidance and perseverance. And thanks to Jacob Weisman and the entire Tachyon Publications team for the care and feeding of Charlie Fish. What a dream to be published by such an incredible press.

JOSH ROUNTREE has published more than sixty stories in a wide variety of magazines and anthologies, including *Beneath Ceaseless Skies, Realms of Fantasy, The Deadlands, Bourbon Penn, PseudoPod, PodCastle, Daily Science Fiction,* and *A Punk Rock Future*. A handful of them have received honorable mentions in *The Year's Best Fantasy and Horror: Seventeenth and Twenty-First Annual Collections*, edited by Ellen Datlow, Kelly Link, and Gavin J. Grant, as well as *The Year's Best Science Fiction: Twenty-Sixth Annual Collection* edited by Gardner Dozois.

His latest short fiction collection is *Fantastic Americana: Stories* from Fairwood Press. Josh lives somewhere in the untamed wilds of Texas, with his wife and children, and tweets about books, records, and guitars at @josh_rountree.